THE RUBY IN THE SMOKE

The
RUBY
in the
SMOKE

Philip Pullman

ALFRED A. KNOPF
New York
22198

Copyright © 1985 by Philip Pullman
Jacket illustration copyright © 1987 by Linda Benson
All rights reserved under International and Pan-American
Copyright Conventions. Published in the United States by
Alfred A. Knopf, Inc., New York. Distributed by Random
House, Inc., New York. Originally published in Great Britain
by Oxford University Press in 1985.

Manufactured in the United States of America
First American Edition
2 4 6 8 10 9 7 5 3 1

Library of Congress Cataloging-in-Publication Data
Pullman, Philip, 1946—   .
The ruby in the smoke.
Summary: In nineteenth-century London, sixteen-year-old
Sally, a recent orphan, becomes involved in a deadly
search for a mysterious ruby.
[1. Mystery and detective stories. 2. Orphans—
Fiction. 3. London—Fiction] I. Title.
PZ7.P968Ru 1987 [Fic] 86-20983
ISBN 0-394-88826-x
ISBN 0-394-98826-4 (lib. bdg.)

Contents

1. The Seven Blessings   3
2. The Web   18
3. The Gentleman of Kent   28
4. The Mutiny   39
5. The Ceremony of the Smoke   44
6. Messages   51
7. The Consequences of Finance   61
8. The Passions of Art   72
9. A Journey to Oxford   86
10. Madame Chang   96
11. The Stereographic Repertory Company   104
12. Substitution   121
13. Lights Below the Water   137
14. Arms and the Girl   153
15. The Turk's Head   163
16. Protecting the Property   170
17. King James's Stairs   179
18. London Bridge   203
19. The East India Docks   215
20. The Clock Tower   222

THE RUBY IN THE SMOKE

1

—•—➤◆➤—•—

The Seven Blessings

ON A COLD, FRETFUL AFTERNOON IN EARLY OCTOBER, 1872, a hansom cab drew up outside the offices of Lockhart and Selby, Shipping Agents, in the financial heart of London, and a young girl got out and paid the driver.

She was a person of sixteen or so—alone, and uncommonly pretty. She was slender and pale, and dressed in mourning, with a black bonnet under which she tucked back a straying twist of blond hair that the wind had teased loose. She had unusually dark brown eyes for one so fair. Her name was Sally Lockhart; and within fifteen minutes, she was going to kill a man.

She stood looking up at the building for a moment and then climbed the three steps and entered. There was a drab corridor facing her, with a porter's office on the right, where an old man sat in front of a fire reading a sensational story of the sort known as a penny dreadful. She tapped on the glass, and he sat up guiltily, thrusting the magazine down beside his chair.

"Beg pardon, miss," he said. "Didn't see yer come in."

"I've come to see Mr. Selby," she said. "But he wasn't expecting me."

3

"Name, please, miss?"

"My name is Lockhart. My father was . . . Mr. Lockhart."

He became friendlier at once.

"Miss Sally, is it? You been here before, miss!"

"Have I? I'm sorry, I don't remember . . ."

"Must've been ten years ago at least. You sat by my fire and had a ginger biscuit and told me all about your pony. You forgotten already? Dear me. . . . I was very sorry to hear about your father, miss. That was a terrible thing, the ship going down like that. He was a real gentleman, miss."

"Yes. . . . Thank you. It was partly about my father that I came. Is Mr. Selby in? Can I see him?"

"Well, I'm afraid he ain't, miss. He's at the West India Docks on business. But Mr. Higgs is here—the company secretary, miss. He'll be glad to talk to you."

"Thank you. I'd better see him, then."

The porter rang a bell, and a young boy appeared, like a sudden solidification of all the grime in the city air. His jacket was torn in three places, his collar had come adrift from the shirt, and his hair looked as if it had been used for an experiment with the powers of electricity.

"What d'yer want?" said this apparition, whose name was Jim.

"Mind yer manners," said the porter. "Take this young lady up to see Mr. Higgs, and smartish. This is Miss Lockhart."

The boy's sharp eyes took her in for a moment, and then flicked back suspiciously to the porter.

"You got my *Union Jack*," he said. "I seen yer hide it when old Higgsy come in earlier."

"I ain't," said the porter, without conviction. "Get on and do as yer told."

"I'll have it," said the boy. "You wait. You ain't stealing my property. Come on then," he added to Sally, and withdrew.

"You'll have to forgive him, Miss Lockhart," said the porter. "He weren't caught young enough to tame, that one."

"I don't mind," said Sally. "Thank you. I'll look in and say good-bye before I go."

The boy was waiting for her at the foot of the staircase.

"Was the boss your old man?" he said as they climbed.

"Yes," she said, meaning to say more, but not finding the words.

"He was a good bloke."

It was a gesture of sympathy, she thought, and felt grateful.

"Do you know anyone called Marchbanks?" she asked. "Is there a Mr. Marchbanks who works here?"

"No. Never heard the name before."

"Or—have you ever heard . . ."

They were near the top of the stairs now, and she stopped to finish the question.

"Have you ever heard of the Seven Blessings?"

"Eh?"

"Please," she said. "It's important."

"No, I ain't," he said. "Sounds like a pub or summat. What is it?"

"It's just something I heard. It's nothing. Forget it, please," she said, and moved up to the top of the stairs. "Where do I find Mr. Higgs?"

"In 'ere," he said, knocking thunderously at a paneled

door. Without waiting for an answer, he opened it and called, "Lady to see Mr. Higgs. Name of Miss Lockhart."

She entered, and the door closed behind her. The room was full of a pompous masculine atmosphere of cigar smoke, leather, dark mahogany, silver inkwells, drawers with brass handles, and glass paperweights. A portly man was trying to roll up a large wall map on the other side of the room and gleaming with effort. His bald pate gleamed, his boots gleamed, the Masonic seal on the heavy gold watch-chain over his paunch gleamed, and his face was shiny with heat and red with years of wine and food.

He finished rolling the map and looked up. His expression became solemn and pious.

"Miss Lockhart? Daughter of the late Matthew Lockhart?"

"Yes," said Sally.

He spread out his hands.

"My dear Miss Lockhart," he said, "I can only say how sorry, how truly sorry, all of us were to hear of your sad loss. A fine man, a generous employer, a Christian gentleman, a gallant soldier, a . . . umm, a great loss, a sad and tragic loss."

She inclined her head.

"You're very kind," she said. "But I wonder if I could ask you something?"

"My dear!" He had become expansive and genial. He pulled out a chair for her and stood with his broad backside to the fire, beaming like an uncle. "Anything that is in my power will be done, I guarantee!"

"Well, it's not that I want anything done—it's simpler than that—it's just . . . Well, did my father ever mention a Mr. Marchbanks? Do you know anyone of that name?"

He appeared to consider the question with great attention. "Marchbanks," he said. "Marchbanks. . . . There is a ship's chandler in Rotherhithe called that—spelled Marjo-ri-banks, you know. Would that be the one? I don't recall your poor father ever having dealings with him, though."

"It may be," said Sally. "Do you know his address?"

"Tasmania Wharf, I believe," said Mr. Higgs.

"Thank you. And there was something else. It sounds silly . . . I shouldn't be bothering you, really, but—"

"My dear Miss Lockhart! Anything that can be done, will be done. Just tell me how I can help."

"Well—have you ever heard the phrase 'the Seven Blessings'?"

Then something extraordinary happened.

Mr. Higgs was a large, well-fed man, as we have remarked; so perhaps it was not Sally's words so much as the years of port, and Cuban cigars, and rich dinners that preceded them which made him crumple at the heart and gasp for air. He took a step forward—then darkness flooded his face, his hands clutched at his waistcoat, and he fell with a crash to the Turkish carpet. One foot kicked and twitched five times, hideously. His open eye was pressed to the carved claw-foot of the chair Sally sat in.

She did not move. Nor did she scream or faint; her only actions were to draw back the hem of her dress from where it brushed the shiny dome of his skull and to breathe deeply, several times, with her eyes shut. Her father had taught her this as a remedy for panic. He had taught her well; it worked.

When she was calm again, she stood up carefully and

stepped away from the body. Her mind was in turmoil, but her hands—she noticed—were perfectly steady. *Good*, she thought. *When I am frightened, I can rely on my hands.* The discovery pleased her absurdly; and then she heard a loud voice in the corridor.

"Samuel Selby, Shipping Agent. Got that?" it said.

"No Mr. Lockhart?" said another voice, more timidly.

"There ain't no Mr. Lockhart. Mr. Lockhart's lying in a hundred fathoms of water in the South China Sea, blast him. I mean, rest his soul. Paint him out, d'ye hear me? Paint him out! And I don't like green. A nice cheerful yeller for me, with them curly lines all 'round. Stylish. Got that?"

"Yes, Mr. Selby," was the muttered reply.

The door opened, and the owner of the loud voice came in. He was a short, stout man with ginger whiskers that clashed unpleasantly with the high color of his cheeks. He looked around—and failed to see the body of Mr. Higgs, which was concealed from him by the broad mahogany desk. Instead, his fierce little eyes rested on Sally.

"Who are you?" he demanded. "Who let you in?"

"The porter," she said.

"What's your name? What d'ye want?"

"I am Sally Lockhart. But—"

"Lockhart?" He gave a low whistle.

"Mr. Selby, I—"

"Where's Higgs? He can deal with you. Higgs! Come out here!"

"Mr. Selby, *he's dead.* . . ."

He fell silent and saw where she was pointing. Then he came around the desk.

"What's going on? When did this happen?"

"A moment ago. We were talking, and suddenly—he fell. Perhaps his heart . . . Mr. Selby, may I sit down?"

"Oh, go on, then. Damn fool. Not you, him. Why can't he have the decency to die on his own floor? I suppose he *is* dead? Have you looked?"

"I don't think he can still be alive."

Mr. Selby hauled the body aside and peered into the dead man's eyes, which stared unpleasantly upward. Sally said nothing.

"Dead as mutton," said Mr. Selby. "Have to call the police now, I suppose. Blast it. What did you want here, anyway? They packed up all your father's stuff and sent it off to the lawyer. There ain't nothing here for you."

Something prompted Sally to be careful. She took out a handkerchief and dabbed at her eyes.

"I—I just wanted to see my father's office," she said.

Mr. Selby grunted suspiciously, then opened the door and yelled downstairs for the porter to call a policeman. A clerk passing the open door with an armful of ledgers looked in, craning his neck. Sally stood up.

"May I leave now?" she said.

"Not likely," said Mr. Selby. "You're a witness, you are. You'll have to have your name and address took, and turn up at the inquest. What d'you want to see the office for, anyway?"

Sally sniffed loudly and dabbed more extravagantly at her eyes. She wondered if she might venture a sob. She wanted to be away and to think, and she was beginning to be afraid of this fierce little man's curiosity. If mentioning the Seven Blessings had really killed Mr. Higgs, she had no wish to risk Mr. Selby's reaction.

But the crying was a good idea. Mr. Selby was not subtle enough to suspect it and waved her away in distaste.

"Oh, go and sit in the porter's room," he said impatiently. "The copper'll want a word with you, but there's no point in hanging about here sniveling. Go on, go downstairs."

She left. On the landing two or three clerks had gathered, and they stared after her with great curiosity.

In the porter's room she found the office boy, reclaiming his penny dreadful from behind the postbox.

" 'S all right," he said. "I won't give yer away. I 'eard yer kill old Higgsy, but I ain't going to tell them."

"I didn't!" she said.

"Course yer did. I 'eard through the door."

"You were listening! That's horrible."

"I didn't mean to. I felt tired all of a sudden, so I leaned against the door, and somehow the words seemed to come through," he said with a grin. "He died o' fright, old Higgsy. Struck dead with terror. Whatever them Seven Blessings is, he knew all right. You better be careful who you ask about it."

She sat down in the porter's chair.

"I just don't know what to do," she said.

"Do about what?"

She looked at his bright eyes and determined face and decided to trust him.

"It's this," she said. "It arrived this morning." She opened her bag and took out a crumpled note. "It was posted from Singapore. That was the last place my father was, before the ship sank. . . . But it's not his writing. I don't know who it's from."

Jim opened it. The note said:

SALI BEWARE OF THE
SEVEN BLESSINGS
MARCHBANKS WILL HELP
CHATTUM
BWARE DARLING

"Blimey," he said. "Tell you what—he can't spell."

"D'you mean my name?"

"What's your name?"

"Sally."

"No. This." He pointed to the word *Chattum.*

"What should it be? Do you know it?"

"C-h-a-t-h-a-m, o' course. Chatham in Kent."

"I suppose it could be."

"An' this Marchbanks lives there. Bet yer. That's why he puts it in. 'Ere," he said, seeing Sally glance upward, "you don't want to worry about old Higgsy. 'Cause if you hadn't said it to him, someone else would've, eventually. He was guilty of something. Hundred to one. And old Selby is too. You ain't said anything to him?"

She shook her head. "Only to you. But I don't even know your name."

"Jim Taylor. And if yer wants to find me, it's Thirteen Fortune Buildings, Clerkenwell. I'll help yer."

"Will you really?"

"You bet."

"Well, if . . . if you hear anything, write to me care of Mr. Temple, of Lincoln's Inn."

The door opened, and the porter came in.

"Are you all right, miss?" he said. "What a terrible thing—here, you," he said to Jim, "stop skulking in here. The copper wants a doctor sent for, to certify the death. Go on, hop it, and find a doctor."

Jim winked at Sally and left. The porter went straight for the postbox and cursed when he found nothing behind it.

"Young blackguard," he muttered. "I might have known it. Would you like a cup o' tea, miss? I don't suppose Mr. Selby thought of that, did he?"

"No, thank you. I ought to be going. My aunt will be getting anxious. . . . Did the policeman want to see me?"

"I expect he will in a minute. He'll come down here when he wants yer. What—er—how was it that Mr. Higgs—"

"We were talking about my father," said Sally, "and he suddenly . . ."

"Weak heart," said the porter. "My brother was took the same way last Christmas. He ate a big dinner and lit a cigar, and then fell face down in the bowl o' nuts. Oh, I beg yer pardon, miss. I don't mean to dwell on it."

Sally shook her head. Presently the policeman came and took her name and address and then left. She stayed a minute or two longer with the old porter; but, remembering Jim's warning, she said nothing to him about the letter from the East Indies. Which was a pity, because he might have been able to tell her something.

SO IT WAS NOT Sally's intention to kill—despite the gun she carried in her bag. The real cause of Mr. Higgs's death, the letter, had arrived only that morning, forwarded by the lawyer to the house in Peveril Square, Islington, where Sally was living. The house belonged to a distant relative of her father's, a grim widow called Mrs. Rees. Sally had been living there since August, and she was unhappy about it. But she had no choice: Mrs. Rees was her only living relative.

Her father had died three months before, when the schooner *Lavinia* had sunk in the South China Sea. He had gone out there to look into some odd discrepancies in the reports from the company's agents in the Far East—something that had to be investigated on the spot and could not be checked from London. He had warned her before he went that it might be dangerous.

"I want to speak to our man in Singapore," he had said. "He's a Dutchman called Van Eeden. I know he's trustworthy. If by some chance I don't come back, he'll be able to tell you why."

"Couldn't you send someone else?"

"No. It's my firm, and I must go myself."

"But Father, you *must* come back!"

"Of course I will. But you must be prepared for—for anything else. I know you'll do it bravely. Keep your powder dry, my dearest, and think of your mother. . . ."

Sally's mother had died during the Indian Mutiny, fifteen years before—shot through the heart by a sepoy's rifle, at the same instant that a bullet from her pistol killed him. Sally was a few months old, their only child. Her mother had been a wild, stormy, romantic young woman, who rode like a Cossack, shot like a champion, and smoked (to the scandal of the fascinated regiment) tiny black cheroots in an ivory holder. She was left-handed, which was why she was holding the pistol in her left hand, which was why she was clasping Sally with the right, which was why the bullet that struck her heart missed the baby; but it grazed her little arm and left a scar. Sally could not remember her mother, but she loved her. And since then she had been brought up by her father—oddly, in the view of various busybodies—but then, Captain Matthew Lockhart's leaving the army to take up the unlikely career of shipping agent was odd enough in itself. Mr. Lockhart taught his daughter himself in the evenings and let her do as she pleased during the day. As a result, her knowledge of English literature, French, history, art, and music was nonexistent, but she had a thorough grounding in the principles of military tactics and bookkeeping, a close acquaintance with the affairs of the stock market, and a working knowledge of Hindustani. Furthermore, she could ride well (though her pony would not agree to the Cossack procedure); and for her fourteenth birthday her father had bought her a little Belgian pistol, the one she carried everywhere, and taught her to shoot. She was now nearly as good a shot as her mother had been. She was solitary, but perfectly happy; the only blight on her childhood was the Nightmare.

This came to her once or twice a year. She would feel herself suffocating in intolerable heat—the darkness was intense—and somewhere nearby, a man's voice was screaming in terrible agony. Then out of the darkness a flickering light would appear, like a candle held by someone hurrying toward her, and another voice would cry, "Look! Look at him! Dear God—look—" But she did not want to look. It was the last thing in the world she wanted to do, and that was the point at which she woke up, drenched in perspiration, suffocating, and sobbing with fear. Her father would come running and calm her down, and presently she would sleep again; but it took a day or so for her to feel free of it.

Then came her father's voyage, the weeks of separation, and finally the telegram telling of his death. At once her father's lawyer, Mr. Temple, had taken charge. The house in Norwood was shut up, the servants paid off, the pony sold. It seemed that there was some irregularity in her father's will, or in the trust he had set up, and that Sally was consequently going to be much poorer than anyone had thought. She was placed in the care of her father's second cousin Mrs. Rees, and there she had lived until this morning, when the letter came.

She thought until she had opened it that it must be from the Dutch agent, Mr. Van Eeden. But the paper was torn, and the writing clumsy and childlike; surely no European businessman would write like that? Besides, it was unsigned. She had gone to her father's office in the hope that someone there would know what it meant.

And she had found that someone did.

She went back to Peveril Square (she did not think of it as home) on the threepenny omnibus and prepared to face Mrs. Rees.

SHE HAD NOT been given a key to the house. This was one of Mrs. Rees's ways of making her feel unwelcome: she had to ring the bell every time she wanted to come in, and the maid who admitted her did so, always, with the air of having been interrupted during some more important task.

"Mrs. Rees is in the drawing room, miss," she said primly. "She says you're to go and see her the minute you get in."

Sally found the lady seated by a thin fire, reading a volume of her late husband's sermons. She did not look up when Sally entered, and Sally looked down at her faded gingery hair and loose, dead-white skin, loathing her. Mrs. Rees was not yet out of her forties, but had found early in life that the role of an aged tyrant suited her well, and played it for all it was worth. She acted as if she were a frail seventy; she had never in her life lifted a finger for herself or had a single kind thought for others, and she welcomed Sally's presence only for the chance it gave her to bully. Sally stood by the fire, waited, and finally spoke.

"I'm sorry I'm late, Mrs. Rees, but I—"

"It is Aunt Caroline, Aunt Caroline," said the lady, her voice whining and creaking irritably. "I have been told by my lawyer that I am your aunt. I did not expect it, I did not seek it, but I shall not shrink from it."

"The maid said you wished to see me, Aunt Caroline."

"I have been applying myself with little success to the subject of your future. Do you intend to remain under my care forever, I wonder? Or would five years be sufficient, or ten? I am merely trying to establish the scale of things. It is plain that you have no prospects, Veronica. I wonder if that had crossed your mind? What accomplishments have you?"

Veronica was Sally's given name. She hated it, but her aunt refused to call her Sally: that was a servant's name, she said. Unable to think of a polite answer, Sally stood mute and found her hands beginning to shake.

"Miss Lockhart is endeavoring to communicate with me by means of thought alone, Ellen," said Mrs. Rees to the maid, who was standing piously inside the door, hands folded and eyes wide with innocence. "I am supposed to understand her without the intervention of language. My education, alas, did not prepare me for such a task; in my day, we used words very frequently among ourselves. We spoke when we were spoken to, for instance."

"I am afraid I have no—accomplishments, Aunt Caroline," said Sally in a low voice.

"None but modesty, you mean to imply? Or is modesty simply the first of a long list? Surely so excellent a gentleman as your late father would not have left you quite unprepared for life?"

Sally shook her head helplessly. The death of Mr. Higgs, and now this . . .

"I thought so," said Mrs. Rees, glinting with a pale triumph. "So even the modest goal of governess is barred to you. We shall have to bend our thoughts to something yet more modest. Possibly one of my friends—Miss Tullett, perhaps, or Mrs. Ringwood—could in charity find room for a lady's companion. I shall make enquiries among them. Ellen, you may bring the tea."

The maid bobbed and left. Sally sat down heavyheartedly, with the prospect of another evening of sarcasm and malice ahead of her, and the knowledge of mystery and danger outside.

2

The Web

SEVERAL DAYS WENT BY. THERE WAS AN INQUEST, which Sally had to attend; Mrs. Rees had arranged (by the merest chance) a visit to her great friend Miss Tullett that morning, and found the inconvenience most vexing. Sally answered the coroner's questions quite truthfully: she had been speaking to Mr. Higgs about her father, she said, when suddenly he had died. No one pressed her closely. She was learning that if she pretended to be weak and frightened, and dabbed at her eyes with a lacy handkerchief, she could turn aside all manner of pressing questions. She disliked this intensely, but she had no other weapons—apart from the pistol. And that was no use against an enemy she could not see.

In any event, no one appeared surprised by the death of Mr. Higgs. A verdict of death by natural causes was returned; the medical evidence had disclosed a weakness of the heart, and the case was dealt with in less than half an hour. Sally went back to Peveril Square; life went back to normal.

But there was a difference. Without knowing it, she had shaken the edge of a web, and the spider at the heart of it had awoken. Now, while she remained unaware (while she sat, in fact, in the uncomfortable drawing room of Miss Tullett and listened to that lady and Mrs. Rees discussing in catlike terms her own shortcomings), three events took place, each of which was to shake the web a little more, and turn the cold eyes of the spider toward London, and toward Sally.

First, a gentleman in a cold house read a newspaper.

Second, an old—what shall we call her? Till we know her better, let us give her the benefit of the doubt, and call her lady—an old lady entertained a lawyer at tea.

Third, a sailor in unhappy circumstances came ashore at the West India Docks and looked for a lodging house.

THE GENTLEMAN in question was called Marchbanks; his servants, in the days when he'd had a full staff, had called him the Major. He lived thirty miles outside London, on the coast of Kent, overlooking a grim tract of land that was flooded at high tide, marshy at low, and desolate always. The house was empty of all but the bare necessities of life, for the Major's wealth had suffered a wasting disease. It was now on the verge of expiring.

On this particular afternoon the Major sat in the bay window of his chilly drawing room. The room faced north, out to the drab wilderness of water; gray and cold as it was, something drew him constantly to this side of the house, to watch the waves and the ships that passed farther out. But he was not looking out to sea just now; he was reading a newspaper lent to him by the only servant who remained—a cook-housekeeper so afflicted by drink and dishonesty that no one else at all would employ her.

Listlessly he turned the pages, holding the paper up to

the fading daylight so as to defer till the last possible moment the expense of lighting the lamps. His eyes scanned the columns of type with no sign of interest or hope—until he caught sight of a story on an inside page which made him sit up suddenly.

The paragraph which interested him most read:

> The only witness to this sad event was Miss Veronica Lockhart, daughter of the late Mr. Matthew Lockhart, a former partner in the firm. Mr. Lockhart's own death, in the wreck of the schooner *Lavinia*, was reported in these pages last August.

He read it twice and rubbed his eyes. Then he got up and went to write a letter.

BEYOND THE TOWER OF LONDON, between St. Katharine's Docks and Shadwell New Basin, lies the area known as Wapping: a district of docks and warehouses, of crumbling tenements and rat-haunted alleys, of narrow streets where the only doors are at second-floor level, surmounted by crude projecting beams and ropes and pulleys. The blind brick walls at pavement level and the brutal-looking apparatus above give the place the air of some hideous dungeon from a nightmare, while the light, filtered and dulled by the grime in the air, seems to come from a long way off—as if through a high window set with bars.

Of all the grim corners of Wapping, none is grimmer than Hangman's Wharf. Its wharfing days are long gone, though the name remains; now it consists of a row of warrenlike houses and shops, their rear rooms actually hanging over the river—a ship's chandler, a pawnbroker's, a pie shop, a pub called the Marquis of Granby, and a lodging house.

Lodgings, in the East End, is a word that covers a multitude of horrors. At its worst, it means a room steaming with damp and poisonous with stench, with a rope stretched across the middle. Those far gone in drink or poverty can pay a penny for the privilege of slumping against this rope, to keep themselves off the floor while they sleep. At its best, it means a decent, clean place where they change the linen as often as they remember. Somewhere in between, there is Holland's Lodgings. There, a bed for the night would cost you threepence, a bed to yourself fourpence, a room to yourself sixpence, and breakfast a penny. You were never alone at Holland's Lodgings. If the fleas disdained your flesh, the bedbugs had no snobbery; they'd take a bite out of anyone.

To this house came Mr. Jeremiah Blyth, a stout and shady lawyer of Hoxton. His previous business with the owner had been transacted elsewhere; this was his first visit to Hangman's Wharf.

His knock brought a child to the door—a girl whose only feature seemed to be, on that dingy afternoon, a pair of enormous, dark eyes. She opened the door a fraction and whispered: "Yessir?"

"Mr. Jeremiah Blyth," said the visitor. "Mrs. Holland is expecting me."

The child opened the door wide enough for him to enter, and then seemed to vanish into the gloom of the hallway.

Mr. Blyth went in, and drummed his fingers on his top hat, and stared at a dusty engraving of the death of Nelson, and tried not to guess at the origin of the stains on the ceiling.

Presently there shuffled in, preceded by the smell of boiled cabbage and old cat, the owner of the house. She was a wizened old woman with sunken cheeks, pinched lips, and glittering eyes. She held out a clawlike hand to her visitor and spoke—but she might have been speaking in Turkish for all the sense Mr. Blyth could make of it.

"I beg your pardon, ma'am? I didn't quite catch . . ."

She crowed and led the way into a tiny parlor, where the smell of old cat had been left to gain depth and maturity. Once the door was shut she opened a little tin box on the mantelpiece and took out a set of false teeth, fitting them into her wrinkled mouth and smacking her lips over them. They were too big for her and looked entirely horrible.

"That's better," she said. "I always forgets me teeth indoors. Me pore dear husband's, these were. Real ivory. Made for him out East twenty-five years ago. Look at the workmanship!"

She bared the brown fangs and gray gums in an animal snarl. Mr. Blyth took a step backward.

"And when he died, pore lamb," she went on, "they was going into the grave with him, being as he was took so quick. Cholera, it was. Gone in a weekend, pore duck. But I whipped 'em out his mouth afore they shut the lid on him. There's years o' wear in them teeth, I thought."

Mr. Blyth gulped.

"There, sit down," she said. "Make yerself at home. Adelaide!"

The child materialized. She could not, thought Mr. Blyth, be older than nine, and so should, by law, have been at school—for the new Board Schools had been set up only two years before, making education compulsory for children under thirteen. However, Mr. Blyth's conscience was as wraithlike as the child herself—far too insubstantial to inquire, let alone protest. So his conscience and the child both remained silent while Mrs. Holland gave directions for tea; and then they both vanished again.

Turning back to her visitor, Mrs. Holland leaned forward, tapped him on the knee, and said, "Well? You got the doings, have yer? Don't be coy, Mr. Blyth. Open yer case, and let an old lady in on the secret."

"Quite, quite," said the lawyer. "Though strictly speaking there is, of course, no secrecy as such, our arrangement being made in perfectly legal terms. . . ."

Mr. Blyth's voice had the habit of fading away rather than coming to a stop at the end of a speech; it seemed to suggest that he was open to any alternative proposal that might be made at the last moment. Mrs. Holland was nodding vigorously.

"That's right," she said. "All square and aboveboard. No hanky-panky—I won't have that. Go on, then, Mr. Blyth."

Mr. Blyth opened his leather case and took out some papers.

"I went down to Swaleness on Wednesday last," he said, "and secured the agreement of the gentleman to the terms we discussed at our last meeting. . . ."

He paused there to let Adelaide enter the room with a tea tray. She put it down on a dusty little table, curtsied to Mrs. Holland, and left without a word. While Mrs. Holland poured the tea, Mr. Blyth resumed.

"The—er—terms. . . . To be sure. The article in question is to be deposited with Hammond and Whitgrove, Bankers, of Winchester Street—"

"The article in question? Don't be coy, Mr. Blyth. Out with it."

He looked exquisitely pained at having to name something clearly. He lowered his voice, leaned forward in his chair, and looked around before he spoke.

"The—ah—ruby will be deposited at Hammond and Whitgrove's bank, to remain there until the death of the gentleman; whereupon, by the terms of his will, duly witnessed by myself and—ah—a Mrs. Thorpe—"

"Who's she? A neighbor?"

"A servant, ma'am. Not entirely reliable—drinks, I understand—but her signature is, of course, valid. Ahem— the ruby will remain, as I say, with Hammond and Whitgrove, until the death of the gentleman; whereupon it will become your property. . . ."

"And that's legal, is it?"

"Perfectly so, Mrs. Holland. . . ."

"No nasty little snags? No last-minute surprises?"

"Nothing of the sort, ma'am. I have here a copy of the document, signed by the gentleman himself. It provides, as you see, for every—ah—eventuality. . . ."

She took the paper from him and scanned it eagerly.

"Seems all right to me," she said. "Very well, Mr. Blyth. I'm a fair woman. You've done a job of work—I'll pay yer fee. What's the damage?"

"Damage, ma'am? Oh—ah—of course. My clerk is preparing an account at the moment, Mrs. Holland. I shall see that it is sent in due course. . . ."

He remained another five minutes or so before leaving. After Adelaide had shown him to the door, making no more noise than a shadow, Mrs. Holland sat for a while in the parlor, reading once again the document that the lawyer had brought her. Then she put away her teeth, after first rinsing them in the teapot, put on her cloak, and set out to look for the premises of Hammond and Whitgrove, Bankers, of Winchester Street.

THE THIRD of our new acquaintances was called Matthew Bedwell. He had been second mate on a tramp ship in the Far East, but that was a year or more ago. At the moment, he was in a sorry state.

He was wandering through the maze of dark streets behind the West India Docks, a kit bag slung over his shoulder, a thin jacket done up tight against the cold.

He had a slip of paper in his pocket with an address on it. From time to time he took this out and checked the name of the street he was in, before putting it back and moving on a little way. Anyone watching him would have thought he was drunk; but there was no smell of alcohol around him, and his speech was not slurred, and his movements were not clumsy. A more compassionate observer would have thought him ill or in pain, and that would have been nearer the mark. But if anyone had seen into his mind and sensed the chaos that reigned in that dark place, they would have thought it remarkable that he managed to keep going at all. There was one idea, flickering dimly like a candle in the swirl of dreams and fears that blew around it. Just one, and it had brought him twelve thousand miles to London—but it was burning very low.

Then something happened that nearly put it out for good.

Bedwell was passing through an alley in Limehouse—a narrow, cobbled place, the bricks black with soot and crumbling with damp—when he caught sight of an open door, with an old man squatting motionless on the step. The old man was Chinese. He was watching Bedwell, and as the sailor came past, he jerked his head slightly and said, "Wantee smoke?"

Bedwell felt every cell in his body strain toward the doorway. He swayed and closed his eyes, and then said, "No. No wantee."

"Good number one smoke," said the Chinaman.

"No. No," repeated Bedwell, and forced himself onward and out of the alley. Once again he consulted his piece of paper; once again he moved forward a hundred yards or so before doing it again. Slowly but surely he made his way west, through Limehouse and Shadwell, until he found himself in Wapping. Another check, and then a pause. The light was fading; he had little strength left. There was a public house nearby, its yellow gleam cheering the drab pavement and drawing him in like a moth.

He paid for a glass of gin and sipped it as if it were medicine—unpleasant but necessary. No, he decided, he could go no farther tonight.

"I'm looking for a lodging house," he said to the barmaid. "Any chance of finding one hereabouts?"

"Two doors along," said the barmaid. "Mrs. Holland's place. But—"

"That'll do," said Bedwell. "Holland. Mrs. Holland. I'll remember that."

He shouldered his kit bag again.

"Are you all right, dearie?" said the barmaid. "You

don't look too good. Treat yerself to another gin, go on."
He shook his head automatically and went out.

Adelaide answered his knock and led him silently to a
room at the back of the house, over the river. The walls
were sodden with damp, the bed was filthy, but he knew
nothing of that. Adelaide gave him a stump of candle and
left him alone, and as soon as the door was shut he fell to
his knees and tore open the kit bag. For the next minute or
so his shaking hands worked busily—and then he lay on
the bed, breathed deeply, and felt everything dissolve and
soak away into oblivion. Very soon, he was lost in a pro-
found sleep. Nothing would awaken him for the best part
of twenty-four hours. He was safe.

But he had nearly given up in Limehouse; the Chinaman, the smoke . . . An opium den, of course. And Bedwell was a slave to the mighty drug.

He slept, and something of great importance to Sally
slept with him.

3

The Gentleman of Kent

THREE NIGHTS LATER, SALLY HAD THE NIGHTMARE again.

And yet it wasn't a nightmare, she felt herself protesting: it was too real. . . .

The terrible heat.

She couldn't move—she was bound hand and foot in the darkness. . . .

Footsteps.

And the screaming, starting so suddenly, and so close to her! Endless screaming and screaming—

The light. Flickering toward her. A face behind it—two faces—blank sheets of white with open, horrified mouths—nothing more—

Voices from the dark: "Look! Look at him! My God—"

And then she woke.

Or rather, surfaced like a swimmer in mortal fear of drowning. She heard herself sobbing and gasping, and remembered: *There's no father. You're alone. You must do without him. You must be strong.*

With an enormous effort she made herself stop crying. She pushed aside the suffocating bedclothes and let the cold night air drench her with chill. Only when she was truly shivering, the nightmare heat gone, did she cover herself again; but it was a long time before she slept.

NEXT MORNING, another letter arrived. She evaded Mrs. Rees as soon as breakfast was over and opened the letter in her bedroom. It had been forwarded by the lawyer, like the previous one, but the stamp was British this time, and the writing educated. She took out the single sheet of cheap paper—and sat up sharply.

> Foreland House
> Kent
> October 10, 1872

Dear Miss Lockhart,

We have not met—you have never heard my name—and only the fact that, many years ago, I knew your father well, could excuse my writing to you. I read in the newspaper of the unfortunate affair at Lockhart and Selby's in the City, and I recalled that Mr. Temple of Lincoln's Inn used to be your father's lawyer. I trust that this letter will reach you. I understand that your father is no more; please accept my deep condolences.

But the fact of his death, and certain circumstances in my own recent affairs, make it necessary for me to speak to you as a matter of urgency. I can say no more at the moment than the three facts that, first, it concerns the Indian Mutiny; second, that an item of incalculable value is involved; and finally, that your personal safety is at present under a deadly threat.

Please, Miss Lockhart, take care, and heed this warning. For the sake of my friendship with your father—for the sake of your own life—come, as soon as you can, and hear what I have to say. There are reasons why I cannot come to you.

Allow me to sign myself as what I have been, without your
knowledge, throughout your life: namely,

Your good friend,
George Marchbanks

Sally read it twice, astonished beyond measure. If her
father and Mr. Marchbanks had been friends, why had
she not heard his name until the letter from the Far East?
And what was this danger?

The Seven Blessings . . .

Of course! He must know what her father had discovered. Her father had written to him, knowing that a letter
would be safe there.

She had a little money in her purse. Putting on her
cloak, she went downstairs quietly and left the house.

SHE SAT in the train, feeling as if she were at the beginning of a military campaign. She was sure that her father
would have planned it coolly, staking out lines of communication and strongholds, forging alliances—well, she
must do the same.

Mr. Marchbanks claimed to be an ally. And, at the very
least, he would be able to tell her something; nothing was
worse than not knowing the threat that hung over you. . . .

She watched the gray edge of the city give way to the
edge of the gray countryside and gazed at the sea to her
left. There were never less than five or six ships visible,
scudding up the Thames estuary before a brisk east wind,
or steaming effortfully down into the teeth of it.

The town of Swaleness was not very large. She decided
not to take a cab from the station but to save her money
and walk, having learned from the porter that Foreland

House was an easy step away, not more than a mile; go along the sea front and then take the river path, he said. She set out at once. The town was cheerless and cold, and the river a muddy creek that wound its way among salt flats before entering that distant line of gray that was the sea. The tide was out; the scene was desolate, with only one human being to be seen.

This was a photographer. He had set up his camera, together with the little portable darkroom that all photographers of the time had to use, right in the center of the narrow path beside the river. He looked like an amiable young man, and since she could see no sign of a foreland, far less a house on it, she decided to ask him the way.

"You're the second person who's passed me already going that way," he said. "The house is over there—a long, low place." He pointed to a grove of stunted trees half a mile farther on.

"Who was the other person?" asked Sally.

"An old woman who looked like one of the witches from *Macbeth*," he said. This allusion was lost on Sally; seeing her puzzlement, he went on. "Wrinkled, don't you know, and hideous, and so forth."

"Oh, I see," she said.

"My card," said the young man. He produced the white slip of pasteboard deftly from nowhere, like a conjurer. It read FREDERICK GARLAND, PHOTOGRAPHIC ARTIST, and gave an address in London. She looked at him again, liking him; his face was humorous, his straw-colored hair stiff and tousled, his expression alert and intelligent.

"Forgive my asking," she said, "but what are you photographing?"

"The landscape," he said. "Not much of one, is it? I

wanted something dismal, d'you see. I'm experimenting with a new combination of chemicals. I've got an idea that it'll be more sensitive in recording this kind of light than the usual stuff."

"Collodion," she said.

"That's right. Are you a photographer?"

"No, but my father used to be interested. . . . Anyway, I must get on. Thank you, Mr. Garland."

He smiled cheerfully and turned back to his camera.

The path curved, following the muddy bank of the river, and finally brought her out behind the grove of trees. There, as the photographer had described it, was the house, covered in peeling stucco, with several tiles missing from the roof; the garden, too, was overgrown and untidy. A more unhappy-looking place she had never seen. She shivered slightly.

She stepped onto the little porch, and was about to ring the bell, when the door opened and a man came out.

He put his finger to his lips and shut the door, taking great care not to make a sound.

"Please," he whispered. "Not a word. This way, quickly . . ."

Sally followed, amazed, as he led her swiftly around the side of the house and into a little glass-paned veranda. He shut the door behind her, listened hard, and then held out his hand.

"Miss Lockhart," he said, "I am Major Marchbanks."

She shook his hand. He was aged; about sixty, she supposed. His complexion was sallow, and his clothes hung loosely on him. His eyes were dark and fine, though sunk in deep hollows. His voice was familiar in some odd way, and there was an intensity in his expression that frightened her, until she realized that he himself was frightened, too: much more than she was.

"Your letter came this morning," she said. "Did my father write and ask you to see me?"

"No . . ." He sounded surprised.

"Then—does the phrase 'the Seven Blessings' mean anything to you?"

It had no effect at all. Major Marchbanks looked blank.

"I'm sorry," he said. "Did you come here to ask me that? I'm so sorry. Did he—your father—"

She told him quickly about her father's last voyage, and about the letter from the East and the death of Mr. Higgs. He put his hand to his brow; he looked utterly crushed and bewildered.

There was a small pine table on the veranda, and a wooden chair by the door. He offered her the chair and then spoke in a low voice.

"I have an enemy, Miss Lockhart, and that enemy is now yours, too. She—it is a woman—is quite, quite evil. She is in this house now, which is why we must hide out here, and why you must leave very soon. Your father—"

"But why? What have I done to her? Who is she?"

"Please—I can't explain now. I shall, believe me. I know nothing of what caused your father's death—nothing of the Seven Blessings, nothing of the South China Sea, nothing of the shipping trade. He could not have known about the evil which has fallen on me, and which now . . . I can't help you. I can do nothing. His trust was misplaced, yet again."

"Again?"

She saw a look of desperate unhappiness cross his face.

It was the look of a man utterly without hope, and it frightened her.

She could only think of the letter from the East. "Did you once live in Chatham?" she said.

"Yes—a long time ago. But please—there's no time. Take this—"

He opened a drawer in the table and took out a package wrapped in brown paper. It was about six inches long, and sealed with string and sealing wax.

"This will tell you everything. Perhaps, since he said nothing to you about it, I shouldn't either. . . . You will have a shock when you read this. Please be ready for it. But your life's in danger whether you know it or not, and at least you'll know why."

She took the package. Her hands were trembling badly; he saw it, and for one strange moment took them both in his and bent his head over them.

Then a door opened.

He sprang away, gray-faced, and a middle-aged woman looked around the door.

"Major—she's on the grounds, sir," she said. "In the garden."

She looked as unhappy as he did, and a strong smell of drink drifted from her. Major Marchbanks beckoned to Sally.

"Through the door," he said. "Thank you, Mrs. Thorpe. Quickly, now . . ."

The woman stood clumsily aside and tried to smile as Sally squeezed past her. The Major led her swiftly through the house; she had an impression of empty rooms, bare floors, echoes and dampness and misery. His fear was catching.

"Please," she said as they reached the front door, "who is this enemy? I don't know anything! You must tell me her name, at least—"

"She's called Mrs. Holland," he whispered, opening the door a crack. He peered through. "Please—I beg you—leave now. You came on foot? You're young, strong, swift—don't wait. Go directly to town. Oh, I'm so sorry. . . . Forgive me. Forgive me."

Those words were so intensely spoken, with a sob in his voice . . .

And she was outside, and the door was shut behind her. Barely ten minutes after she had arrived, she was leaving again. She looked up at the blank, peeling wall of the house and thought: *Is this enemy watching?*

She set off along the weed-covered drive, past the grove of dark trees, and back onto the track by the river. The tide was coming in; a sluggish flow stirred the edges of the muddy river. There was no sign of the photographer, unfortunately. The landscape was utterly bare.

She hurried onward, very conscious of the package in her bag. Halfway along the riverbank, she stopped and looked back. What made her look she did not know, but she saw a small figure rounding the trees—a woman dressed in black. An old woman. She was too far away to see plainly, but she was hurrying after Sally. Her little black shape was the only purposeful element in all that gray wilderness.

Sally hastened on until she reached the main road, and looked back again. It was as if the little black figure was coming in with the tide; she was no farther behind, and even seemed to be gaining. Where could Sally hide?

The road to the town curved around slightly, away

from the sea, and she thought that if she were to take a side road while she was out of sight, she might—

Then she saw something better still. The photographer stood on the seafront, beside his little tent, consulting an instrument of some sort. She looked back—the little black figure was hidden by the end of the terrace of seafront houses. She ran up to the photographer, who looked up in surprise, and then grinned with pleasure.

"It's you," he said.

"Please," she said, "can you help me?"

"Of course. Glad to. What can I do?"

"I'm being followed. That old woman—she's after me. She's dangerous. I don't know what to do."

His eyes sparkled with pleasure.

"In the tent," he said, lifting the flap. "Don't move, or you'll knock things over. Never mind the smell."

She did as he said, and he dropped the flap and laced it up. The smell was fierce—something like smelling salts. It was completely dark.

"Don't speak," he said quietly. "I'll tell you when she's gone. My word, here she comes now. She's crossing the road. Coming toward us . . ."

Sally stood motionless, listening to the crying of the gulls, the clip-clop of horses and trundle of wheels as a carriage went along the road, and then the sharp, swift tread of a pair of nailed boots. It stopped only a yard or so away.

"Excuse me, sir," said a voice, an old voice that seemed to wheeze and click in an odd way.

"Mmm? What is it?" Garland's voice was muffled. "Wait a moment. I'm composing a picture. Can't come out from under the cloth till it's ready. . . . There," he said more clearly. "Well, ma'am?"

"Have you seen a young girl come this way, sir? A girl dressed in black?"

"Yes, I have. Devil of a hurry. Remarkably pretty girl—blond—would that be the one?"

"Trust a handsome gentleman like you to notice that, sir! Yes, she's the one, bless her. Did you see which way she went?"

"As a matter of fact, she asked me the way to the Swan. Said she wanted the Ramsgate coach. I told her she had ten minutes to catch it."

"The Swan, sir? Where might that be?"

He gave directions, and the old woman thanked him and set off.

"Don't move," he said in a low voice. "She hasn't turned the corner yet. 'Fraid you'll have to stay among the stinks for a while."

"Thank you," she said formally. "Though you need not have tried to flatter me."

"Oh, dear. All right, I take it back. You're almost as ugly as she is. Look, what *is* going on?"

"I just don't know. I'm all mixed up in something horrible. I can't tell you what it is—"

"Shhh!"

Footsteps approached slowly, passed the tent, and faded away.

"Fat man with a dog," he said. "Gone now."

"Is she out of sight?"

"Yes, she's vanished. To Ramsgate, with any luck."

"May I come out?"

He unlaced the flap and held it open.

"Thank you," she said. "May I pay you for the use of your tent?"

His eyes opened wide. For a moment she thought he

was going to laugh, but he politely declined. She felt her-self beginning to blush; she should not have offered money. She turned away swiftly.

"Don't go," he said. "I don't even know your name. That payment I will exact."

"Sally Lockhart," she said, staring out to sea. "I'm sorry. I didn't mean to insult you. But—"

"I'm not insulted at all. But you can't expect to pay for everything, you know. What are you going to do now?"

She felt like a child. It was not a sensation she enjoyed.

"I'm going back to London," she said. "I expect I shall manage to avoid her. Good-bye."

"Would you like a companion? I've nearly finished here in any case, and if that old weasel is dangerous—"

"No, thank you. I must be going."

She walked away. She would have loved his company, but she would never have admitted it. She felt somehow that the pretense of helplessness, which worked so well with other men, would not take him in for a moment. That was why she had offered to pay him: she wanted to meet him on equal terms. But that had gone wrong too. She felt as if she knew nothing and could do nothing cor-rectly, and she felt quite alone.

4

The Mutiny

THERE WAS NO SIGN OF THE OLD WOMAN AT THE STA-
tion. The only other passengers were a parson and his
wife, three or four soldiers, and a mother with two children. Sally found an empty compartment without difficulty.

She waited until the train was out of the station before
she opened the parcel. The knots were carefully buried in
sealing wax, and she broke a fingernail trying to scrape it
away.

Finally she had it open and discovered a book.

It looked like a diary of some sort. It was quite thick,
and the pages were covered in close writing. It had been
roughly bound in gray cardboard, but the stitching was
loose, and one whole section fell out in her hand. She replaced it carefully and began to read.

The first page bore this inscription: *A Narrative of the
Events in Lucknow and Agrapur, India, 1856–7; with an
account of the disappearance of the Ruby of Agrapur,
and the part played by the child known as Sally Lockhart.*

She stopped and read it again. Herself! And a ruby—

A hundred questions rose suddenly like flies disturbed

39

at a feast, and filled her head with confusion. She closed her eyes and waited for calm, then opened them and read on.

In 1856, I, George Arthur Marchbanks, was serving with the Duke of Cornwall's Light Infantry, the Thirty-second Foot, at Agrapur in the province of Oudh. Some months before the outbreak of the mutiny, I had occasion to visit the Maharajah of Agrapur in company with three of my brother officers, namely Colonel Brandon, Major Park, and Captain Lockhart.

The visit was ostensibly a private one for the purpose of sport. In fact, however, our main purpose was to conduct certain secret political discussions with the maharajah. The content of these discussions need not concern this account, except insofar as they contributed to the suspicion in which the maharajah was held by one faction of his subjects—a suspicion which led, as I shall show, to his fate during the terrible events of the following year.

On the second evening of our visit to Agrapur, the maharajah gave a banquet in our honor. Whether or not it was his intention to impress us with his wealth, that was certainly the effect; for I had never set eyes upon so prodigal a display of splendor as that which met us that evening.

The banquet room was set about with pillars of marble exquisitely carved, and bearing at their capitals representations of the lotus flower, lavishly covered in gold leaf. The floor we trod on was set with lapis lazuli and onyx; a fountain in the corner tinkled with rose-scented water, and the maharajah's court musicians played their strange, languid melodies behind a screen of inlaid mahogany. The dishes were of solid gold; but the centerpiece of the display was the ruby, of incomparable size and luster, which gleamed at the maharajah's breast.

This was the famous Ruby of Agrapur, about which I had heard a good deal. I could not help gazing at it—I confess that something in its depth and beauty, in the blood-red liquid fire that seemed to fill it, fascinated me and held my attention, so that I stared more than was strictly polite; in any event, the maharajah noticed my curiosity and told us the story of the stone.

It had been discovered in Burma six centuries before, and been given in tribute to Balban, King of Delhi, from whom it had descended to the princely house of Agrapur. Throughout the centuries it had been lost, stolen, sold, given in ransom countless times, and had always returned to its royal owners. It had been responsible for deaths too many to list— murders, suicides, executions—and once it had been the cause of a war in which the population of an entire province had been put to the sword. Less than fifty years before, it had been stolen by a French adventurer. He, poor wretch, thought to escape detection by swallowing it, but in vain: he was torn open while still alive, and the stone plucked warm from his belly.

The maharajah's eyes met mine as he recounted these tales.

"Would you care to examine it, Major?" he asked. "Hold it close to the light and look inside. But take care that you do not fall!"

He handed it to me, and I did as he suggested. As the lamplight fell on the stone, a strange phenomenon took place: the red glow at the heart of it seemed to swirl and part like smoke, to reveal a series of ledges and chasms—a fantastic landscape of gorges, peaks, and terrifying abysses whose depth was impossible to plumb. Only once have I read of such a landscape, and that was in a work on the delusions and horrors of opium addiction.

The effect of this extraordinary sight was what the maharajah had predicted. I swayed, suddenly struck by the most dizzying vertigo. Captain Lockhart caught my arm, and the maharajah took back the stone, laughing. The incident was passed off with a joke.

Our visit ended shortly afterward. I did not see the maharajah again for a year or so, and then only in the course of the horrible event which forms the climax of this narrative— an event which has brought me more shame and unhappiness than I would have imagined possible. May God (if there is a God, and not an infinity of mocking demons) grant me oblivion and forgetfulness, and may it come soon!

The year which passed after I first saw the stone was a time of omens and portents—signs of the terrible storm which was about to break over us in the mutiny, and signs which, to a man, we failed to read. On the horrors and savagery of the mutiny itself it is not my present concern to dwell. Others more eloquent than I have told the story of this time, with its deeds of heroism shining like beacons amid scenes of hideous carnage; it is enough to say that, while hundreds did not survive, I did—and so did three others in whose destiny the ruby continues to play a large and commanding part.

I pass on now to a time during the Siege of Lucknow, not long before its relief.

My regiment was garrisoned in the city, and . . .

Sally looked up. The train had drawn into a station; she saw a sign that read CHATHAM. She shut the book, her head filled with strange images: a golden banquet, hideous deaths, and a stone that intoxicated like opium. . . . "Three others" had survived, said the Major; her father and herself, she thought at once. And the third?

She opened the book again—only to shut it hastily as the carriage door opened and a man got in.

He was jauntily dressed in a bright, checkered suit, with a gaudy pin in his cravat. He lifted his bowler hat to Sally before sitting down.

"Afternoon, miss," he said.

"Good afternoon."

She looked away, out of the opposite window. She did not want conversation, and there was something about this man's familiar smile she did not like. Girls of Sally's class did not travel alone; it looked odd and invited the wrong kind of attention.

The train steamed out of the station, and the man took out a packet of sandwiches and started to eat. He took no more notice of her. She sat still, gazing out at the marshes, the city in the distance, and the masts of ships in the docks and shipyards far off to the right.

Time passed. Eventually the train drew in at London Bridge Station, under the dark, smoky canopy of glass, and the sound of the engine changed as the steam hissed and echoed amid the calls of the porters and the clanging of the jolting carriages. Sally sat up and rubbed her eyes. She had fallen asleep.

The door of the compartment was swinging open.

The man had gone, and so had the book. He had stolen it and vanished.

5

The Ceremony of the Smoke

SHE LEAPED UP IN ALARM AND SPRANG TO THE DOOR. But the platform was crowded, and the only things she remembered about the man were his checkered suit and bowler hat—and there were dozens of those in sight. . . .

A wave of despair passed over her. To lose that book— her own past was in those pages! It was the key to everything. . . .

She turned back to the compartment. Her bag lay in the corner where she had sat. She bent to pick it up and then noticed, on the floor under the edge of the seat, a few sheets of paper.

The book had been loosely bound; these pages must have fallen out and dropped while she was asleep. The thief hadn't noticed them!

Most of them were blank, but on one there were a few lines of writing, continued from a previous sheet, which said:

> . . . a place of darkness, under a knotted rope. Three red lights shine clearly on the spot when the moon pulls on the water. Take it. It is clearly yours by my gift, and by the laws of England. *Antequam haec legis, mortuus ero; utinam ex animo hominum tam celeriter memoria mea discedat.*

Sally, who knew no Latin, folded the paper and put it in her bag; and then, sick with disappointment, set out for Mrs. Rees's.

MEANWHILE, in Wapping, a sinister little ceremony was taking place.

Once a day, on Mrs. Holland's orders, Adelaide took up a bowl of soup to the gentleman on the second floor. Mrs. Holland had discovered Matthew Bedwell's craving very early, and, never slow to take up an opportunity, found her venomous old curiosity powerfully aroused.

For her guest had fragments of a very interesting story to tell. He was delirious, alternately sweating with pain and raving at the visions which crowded in from the dirty walls. Mrs. Holland listened patiently, supplied a little of the drug, listened again, and provided more opium in exchange for details about the things he said in his madness. Little by little the story emerged—and Mrs. Holland realized that she was sitting on a fortune.

Bedwell's tale concerned the affairs of Lockhart and Selby, Shipping Agents. Mrs. Holland's ears pricked up when they heard the name Lockhart: she had her own interest in that family, and the coincidence astonished her. But as the tale came out, she realized that this was a new angle altogether: the loss of the schooner *Lavinia*, the death of the owner, the firm's unusually high profits from their China trade, and a hundred and one things besides. Mrs. Holland, though not a superstitious woman, blessed the hand of Providence.

As for Bedwell, he was too helpless to move. Mrs. Holland was not quite sure that she had extracted all the knowledge that lay fuming in his brain—which was why she kept him alive, if he could be said to be living. As soon as she decided that the back bedroom was needed for some other purpose, Death and Bedwell, who had missed each other in the South China Sea, could finally keep their rendezvous in the Thames. An appropriate address, Hangman's Wharf.

So now Adelaide, having ladled a quantity of warm, greasy soup into a bowl, clumsily hacked a slice of bread to go with it and climbed the stairs to the back bedroom. There was silence from inside; she hoped he was asleep. She unlocked the door and held her breath, loathing the stale, heavy air and the damp chill that struck her as she entered.

The gentleman was lying on the mattress with a rough blanket up to his chest, but he was not asleep. His eyes followed her as she put the bowl down on a nearby chair.

"Adelaide," he whispered.

"Yessir?"

"What you got there?"

"Soup, sir. Mrs. Holland says you got to eat it up 'cause it'll do you good."

"You got a pipe for me?"

"After the soup, sir."

She did not look at him; they both spoke in whispers. He raised himself on one elbow and then struggled painfully upright, and she stood back against the wall as if she had no substance at all—as if she were a shadow. Only her huge eyes seemed alive.

"Give us it here," he said.

She took him the bowl and crumbled the bread into it for him, and then went to the far wall as he ate. But he had no appetite; after a couple of spoonfuls he pushed it away.

"Don't want it," he said. "There's no goodness in it. Where's the pipe?"

"You got to eat it, sir, 'cause Mrs. Holland'll kill me else," said Adelaide. "Please . . ."

"You eat it. You could do with a feed," he said. "Come on, Adelaide. The pipe, girl."

Reluctantly she opened the cupboard which, with the chair and the bed, was the only furniture the room possessed, and took out a long, heavy pipe, jointed in three sections. He watched intently as she fitted it together, laid it on the bed beside him, and cut a small piece of brown gum from a lump in the cupboard.

"Lie down," she said. "It sends you off quick, now. You gotta lie down else you'll fall."

He did as the little girl said, stretching out languorously on his side. The chilly gray light of the fading afternoon, struggling through the grime on the tiny window, gave the scene the somber color of a steel engraving. An insect crawled lethargically across the greasy pillow as Adelaide applied a lighted match to the lump of opium. She passed the drug, transfixed on a pin, to and fro across the flame until it began to bubble and the fumes leaked outward. Bedwell sucked at the mouthpiece, and as Adelaide held the opium above the bowl, the sweet, heady smoke was dragged into the pipe.

When it had stopped smoking, she lit another match and repeated the process. She hated it. She hated what it did to him, because it made her think that under every human face there was the face of a staring, dribbling, helpless idiot.

"More," he mumbled.

"There ain't no more," she whispered.

"Come on, Adelaide," he whined. "More."

"One more, then."

Again she struck a match; again the opium bubbled and fumed. The smoke poured into the bowl like a river disappearing underground. Adelaide shook out the match and dropped it with its fellows on the floor.

He breathed a long sigh. The fumes were thick in the room now, making her feel dizzy.

"D'you know, I haven't got the strength to get up and leave?" he said.

"No, sir," she whispered.

A strange thing happened to his voice when he was in the opium trance: it lost the rough sailor's edge and became refined and even gentle.

"I think about it, though. Day and night. Oh, Adelaide . . . the Seven Blessings! No, no! You fiends—devils—leave me—"

He was starting to rave. Adelaide sat as far away from him as she could; she dared not leave, for fear Mrs. Holland would ask her what the gentleman had said, and yet she feared to stay, for his words brought nightmares to her. The Seven Blessings—this phrase had come twice lately, and each time with terror.

He stopped in midsentence. Suddenly his expression changed and became lucid and confiding.

"Lockhart," he said. "I remember now. Adelaide, are you there?"

"Yessir," she whispered.

"Try to remember something for me—will you?"

"Yessir."

"A man called Lockhart . . . asked me to find his daughter. A girl called Sally. I've got a message for her. Very important. . . . Could you find her for me?"

"I dunno, sir."

"London's a big place. Perhaps you couldn't."

"I could try, sir."

"Good girl. Oh, dear God, what am I doing?" he went on helplessly. "Look at me. As weak as a baby.... What would my brother say?"

"You got a brother, sir?"

The light had almost gone now; she looked like a mother by the bed of her sick child, seen through the distorting haze of opium. She reached across and mopped his face with the filthy sheet, and he seized her hand gratefully.

"A fine man," he mumbled. "My twin. Identical. The same body, but his spirit's all light, Adelaide, while mine's corruption and darkness. He's a clergyman. Nicholas. The Reverend Nicholas Bedwell.... Have you any brothers or sisters?"

"No, sir. I ain't got any."

"Your mother alive? Your father?"

"I ain't got a mother. I got a father, though. He's a recruiting sergeant."

This was a lie. Adelaide's father had been anonymous even to her mother, who herself had vanished a fortnight after the birth; but Adelaide had invented a father, and formed him in the image of the most splendid and gallant men her stunted life had ever seen. One of the these swaggering figures, jaunty little pillbox hat cocked, glass in hand, had once winked at her as he stood with his fellows outside a public house and laughed loudly at some coarse jest. She hadn't heard the jest. All she had retained was an image of heroic male splendor falling suddenly into her dark little life like a shaft of sunlight. That wink had begotten a father upon his own daughter.

"Fine men," muttered Bedwell. "Fine body of men."
His eyes closed.

"Go to sleep, sir," she whispered.

"Don't tell her, Adelaide. Don't tell her about—what I said. She's an evil woman."

"Yes, sir. . . ."

Then he began to rave again, and the room filled up with ghosts and Chinese demons and visions of torture and poisoned ecstasy, and abysses yawned sickeningly below. Adelaide sat in the darkness, holding his hand and thinking.

6

Messages

SINCE THE DEATH OF MR. HIGGS, LIFE AT THE OFFICE had grown dull. The feud between the porter and Jim the office boy had petered out, the porter having run out of hiding places and Jim having run out of penny magazines; he had nothing better to do that afternoon, in fact, than to flick bits of paper, with an India rubber band, at the portrait of Queen Victoria over the fireplace of the porter's room.

When Adelaide arrived and tapped on the glass, Jim took no notice at first. He was busy improving his aim. The old man opened the window and said, "Yus? What d'yer want?"

"Miss Lockhart," whispered Adelaide.

Jim heard and looked up.

"Miss Lockhart?" said the porter. "You sure?"

She nodded.

"What d'you want her for?" said Jim.

"Never you mind, you weevil," said the old man.

Jim flicked a scrap of paper at the porter's head and dodged the frail blow aimed at him in return.

"If you got a message for Miss Lockhart, I'll take it," he said. "Come out here a minute."

He took Adelaide to the foot of the stairs, out of earshot of the porter.

"What's yer name?" he said.

"Adelaide."

"What d'yer want Miss Lockhart for?"

"I dunno."

"Well, who sent yer?"

"A gentleman."

He bent closer to hear what she said, becoming conscious of the aroma of Holland's Lodgings about her clothes, and of dirty child about her. But he wasn't fussy, and he had remembered something important.

"Did you ever hear," he said, "of something called the Seven Blessings?"

In the past fortnight he had asked that of all kinds of people, except Mr. Selby; and he had always got the same response—no, they hadn't.

But she had. She was frightened. She seemed to shrink inside her cloak, and her eyes became darker than ever.

"What of it?" she whispered.

"You have, ain't yer?"

She nodded.

"Well, what is it?" he went on. "It's important."

"I dunno."

"Where d'you hear of it?"

She twisted her mouth and looked away. Two clerks came out of their office at the top of the stairs and saw them.

" 'Ere," said one of them. "Look at young Jim courting."

"Who's yer ladylove, Jim?" called the other.

Jim looked up and released a jet of language that might

have blistered a battleship. He was no respecter of clerks: they were a very low form of life.

"Never mind them," he said to Adelaide. "Listen—you got to tell me about the Seven Blessings. There's a man died in here because of that."

He told her what had happened. She did not look up, but her eyes widened.

"I've got to look for Miss Lockhart, 'cause he said so," she said when he'd finished. "Only I mustn't tell Mrs. Holland, else she'll kill me."

"Well, tell me what he bloody said! Go on!"

She did—haltingly, little by little, for she had nothing of Jim's fluency, and she was so unused to being listened to that she hardly knew how loudly to speak. Jim had to prompt her to repeat much of it.

"Right," he said eventually. "I'll fetch Miss Lockhart, and you can talk to her. All right?"

"I can't," she said. "I can't never get away except when Mrs. Holland sends me out. She'll kill me."

"Course she won't bleeding kill yer! You'll have to come out, else—"

"I *can't,*" she said. "She killed the last little girl she had. She took all her bones out. She told me."

"Well, how are you going to find Miss Lockhart, then?"

"I dunno."

"Oh, blimey. Well, look—I'll come through Wapping each night on me way home, and you meet me somewhere and tell me what's happened. Where can you meet me?"

She looked down, twisting her mouth, thinking.

"By the Old Stairs," she said.

"All right. By the Old Stairs, every night, half-past six."

"I gotta go now," she said.
"Don't forget," he called. "Half-past six."
But Adelaide had vanished.

> 13 Fortune Buildings
> Chandler's Row
> Clerkenwell
> Friday 25 October 1872

Miss S. Lockhart
9 Peveril Square
Islington

Dear Miss Lockhart,
   I beg to inform you that I have discovered something about the Seven (7) Blessings. There is a gentleman called Mr. Bedwell at present situated at Holland's Lodgings, Hangman's Wharf, Wapping, he has been taking opium and talking about you. He has also said the Seven Blessings but I do not know what it means. The landlady is Mrs. Holland, she is not to be trusted. If you come to the bandstand in the Clerkenwell Gardens tomorrow at half-past two I can tell you more.

> I beg to remain,
> Your humble and obedient servant,
> J. Taylor, Esquire (Jim)

Thus wrote Jim, after the best models of clerkly correspondence. He posted the letter on Friday, in the confident expectation (this *was* the nineteenth century, after all) of its being delivered before the day was out, and of Sally's tomorrow being the same as his.

Holland's Lodgings
Hangman's Wharf
Wapping
25 October 1872

Samuel Selby, Esquire
Lockhart and Selby
Cheapside
London

Dear Mr. Selby,

I have the honor to represent a gentleman, who has certain information, concerning your enterprises in the East, this gentleman wishes it known, that he will be obliged to publish what he knows in the papers, unless certain conditions is agreed to. As a sample of his knowledge he has asked me to mention the schooner *Lavinia*, and a sailor named Ah Ling. Hoping this proposal is agreeable to you, and this finds you as it leaves me,

Yours truly,
M. Holland (Mrs.)

P.S. An early reply would be appreciated by all.

Thus wrote Mrs. Holland, after a particularly interesting afternoon with Bedwell, the drug, and her pencil and paper.

SALLY STOOD under the inadequate shelter of a nearly bare lime tree in Clerkenwell Gardens and waited for Jim. The rain had already soaked her cloak and hat, and was now insinuating itself down her neck. In order to come out at all she had had to disobey Mrs. Rees; she dreaded the reception that awaited her return.

But she did not have long to wait. Presently Jim came running, even wetter than she was, and tugged her over to the empty bandstand that stood on a patch of soggy grass.

"Under 'ere," he said, lifting a loose panel in the side of the little stage.

He dived into the gloom like a ferret. She followed him more carefully through the tunnels of folding chairs and arrived at a cavelike hollow where he was already lighting a stump of candle.

She settled down opposite him. The floor was dusty but dry, and the rain drummed on the stage overhead as he set the candle carefully upright between them.

"Well?" he said. "D'you want to hear, or not?"

"Of course I do!"

Jim repeated all that Adelaide had told him, but more crisply. He was good with words: the penny dreadfuls had taught him well.

"What d'you think of that, then?" he said when he came to the end.

"Jim, it must be right! Mrs. Holland—it's the woman Major Marchbanks told me about. Yesterday, in Kent—"

She told him what had happened.

"A ruby," he said, awestruck.

"But I don't see how it ties in with the rest of it. I mean, Major Marchbanks had never heard of the Seven Blessings."

"And this bloke of Adelaide's never said nothing about a ruby. Maybe there's two mysteries, and not one. Maybe there's no connection."

"But there *is* a connection," said Sally. "Me."

"And Mrs. Holland."

There was a pause. "I'll have to see him," said Sally.

"You can't. Not while Mrs. Holland's got him. Oh, yeah! I forgot—he's got a brother who's a parson. His name's Nicholas. They're twins."

"The Reverend Nicholas Bedwell," said Sally. "I wonder if we could find him. Perhaps he could get his brother out. . . ."

"He's a slave to opium," said Jim. "And Adelaide says he's terrified of Chinamen. Whenever he sees a Chinaman in his visions, he screams."

They fell silent for a moment.

"I wish I hadn't lost that book," said Sally.

"You never lost it. She had it pinched."

"She did? But it was a man. He got in at Chatham."

"Why would anyone want a scruffy old book unless they knew what was in it? Of course it was her doing."

Sally blinked. Why hadn't she made this connection? But once he had said it, it was obvious.

"So she's got the book," she said. "Jim, it's going to drive me mad! What on earth does she want it for?"

"You ain't half slow," he said severely. "It's that ruby she wants. What's it say on them bits o' paper he left behind?"

She showed him the loose pages she'd found in the train.

"There you are. 'Take it,' he says. He's hidden it somewhere away from her, and he's telling you where it is. And I'll tell you something, and all—if she wants the ruby, she'll be back for this."

ON THE following evening, three people sat in the kitchen at Holland's Lodgings, where a filthy iron stove gave off a tropical glow. One of the three was Adelaide, and Adelaide didn't count; she sat, disregarded, in the corner. Mrs. Holland sat at the table, turning the leaves of Major Marchbanks's book. The third person was a visitor, seated in the armchair by the stove, alternately sipping a mug of tea and mopping his brow. He wore a bright, checkered suit. There was a brown bowler hat pushed back on his head, and a sparkling pin in his cravat.

Sally would have recognized him, for he was the man from the train. He often did little jobs for Mrs. Holland—anything that needed light fingers or a persuasive manner was meat and drink to Henry Hopkins. He'd gone with her to Swaleness, lurked about in the town while she went out to Foreland House, and then (after a hurried conference by the Ramsgate coach) run back to the station just in case Sally had gone that way after all. Which, of course, she had. Mr. Hopkins had boarded the train, too—waited a station or so before getting into Sally's compartment—and then plied his trade, with the results that now lay on Mrs. Holland's bony knees.

Patting her fangs into place, the lady spoke.

"Nice job o' work, Mr. Hopkins," she said. "Very neatly done."

"Dead easy," said the visitor modestly. "She fell asleep, see. All I had to do was lift it off her little lap."

"Very nice...." Mrs. Holland said again, and turned another page.

Mr. Hopkins took another sip of tea.

"That—er—curious, is it, that book?" he said.

"Not to me," said Mrs. Holland. "I know this story off my heart."

"Oh?" said Mr. Hopkins carefully.

"But it'd be news to that young lady. I daresay that if she was to read this, it'd be a first-rate disaster."

"Oh, really?"

"So I think she better have an accident."

Silence. He shifted uncomfortably in his chair.

"Well," he said at length, "I ain't sure as I wants to know about that, Mrs. Holland."

"And I ain't sure as you've got much choice, Mr. Hopkins," she said, flicking through the book. "Dear me, these pages is terrible loose. I hope you didn't lose none of 'em."

"I don't understand, Mrs. H. I ain't got much choice about what?"

But she had stopped listening. Her ancient eyes narrowed; she read the last page of the book, turned back, flicked through the rest, read it again, held the book up and shook it, and finally flung it down with a curse.

Mr. Hopkins backed away nervously.

"What's the matter?" he said.

"That bleedin' legal earwig," she snarled. "That great mumblin' misery, to let hisself be fooled like that . . ."

"Who're you talking about?" said Henry Hopkins.

"A drivelin' snivelin' nitwit of a lawyer up in Hoxton. Name of Blyth. By God, Mr. Hopkins, he'll have a clear idea of his shortcomings when I'm through with him. . . . And as for you," she went on venomously, "I seen tailors' dummies with more sense than you, you oily popinjay."

"Me? What've I done?"

"You gone and lost the most important page in the whole bleedin' book!"

"I thought you said as how you knew it all by heart, ma'am?"

She thrust the book at him.

"Read this, if yer can. Read it!"

Her horny old finger jabbed at the last paragraph in the book. He read it aloud.

" 'I have therefore withdrawn the ruby from the bank. It is the only chance I have of redeeming myself and saving something from the wreck of my life. The will I made, under the directions of that woman, has been annulled; her lawyer failed to foresee a way out of the contract I signed. I shall die intestate. But I mean you to have the stone. I have hidden it, and to make doubly sure, I shall conceal its whereabouts in a cipher. It is in—' "

There was no more. He stopped and looked at her.

"Yes, Mr. Hopkins," she said, smiling horribly. "You see what you done?"

He quailed.

"It weren't in the book, ma'am," he said. "I swear it!"

"I said something about an accident, didn't I?"

He gulped. "Well, like I say, I—"

"Oh, you'll manage a little accident for her. You'll do that all right, Mr. Hopkins. One look at the paper tomorrow, and you'll do whatever I want."

"What d'you mean by that?"

"Wait and see," she said. "You're going to get that piece of paper—she'll have it somewhere—and then you're going to finish her off."

He blinked.

"I ain't," he said unhappily.

"Oh, you are, Mr. Hopkins. You take my word for it."

7

The Consequences of Finance

IT DID NOT TAKE MR. HOPKINS LONG TO FIND THE
story in the newspaper. It seemed to leap out of the page
at him, accompanied by alarm bells, police whistles, and
the clink of handcuffs.

MYSTERIOUS DEATH OF RETIRED MAJOR

A SURVIVOR OF THE MUTINY

HOUSEKEEPER TELLS OF "MAN IN CHECKERED SUIT"

The Kent Police were alerted this morning to the mysterious death of Major George Marchbanks, of Foreland
House, Swaleness.

His body was discovered by his housekeeper, Mrs.
Thorpe, in the library of his isolated dwelling. He had apparently been shot. An empty pistol was found nearby.

The Major lived a retired life, and his housekeeper was
his only servant. According to a statement made by Su-
perintendent Hewitt of the Kent Constabulary, the police
are anxious to trace a man in a checkered suit, with a
bowler hat and a diamond pin. This man visited Major

Marchbanks on the morning of his death, when it is believed that an altercation took place.

Major Marchbanks was a widower, with no surviving family. He served in India for many years. . . .

Mr. Hopkins was overcome with rage and had to sit down and catch his breath.

"You old crab," he muttered. "You spider. You calculating old bitch. I'll . . ."

But he was caught, and he knew it. If he failed to do as she wanted, Mrs. Holland would manufacture some cast-iron evidence that would send him to the gallows for a murder he didn't commit. He sighed heavily and went at once to change his clothes to a new serge suit in dark blue, wondering what this game was that Mrs. Holland was playing. If murder was one of the stakes, what must the prize be worth?

MRS. REES'S MAID Ellen hated Sally, and didn't know why. Spite and envy were at the bottom of it, and the whole bundle of feelings was so uncomfortable that when she was offered a justification for her antipathy, she seized it at once without examining it too closely.

This justification was provided by Mr. Hopkins. Mrs. Holland had ferreted Sally's address out of the lawyer's clerk, and Mr. Hopkins's smoothness of manner did the rest. He represented himself to Ellen as a police detective and told her that Sally was a thief who had stolen some letters: a matter of such delicacy—family very highly connected—the slightest breath of scandal—the noblest in the land, and so on. All that, of course, meant nothing, but it was the sort of thing that filled the pages of the magazines that Ellen read, and she lapped it up at once.

Their conversation took place on the area steps. She was very soon persuaded that her duty to herself, her mistress, and her country lay in admitting Mr. Hopkins secretly to the house after everyone had gone to bed. Accordingly, toward midnight, she opened the kitchen door, and Mr. Hopkins, fortified by a quantity of brandy, found his way upstairs to the door of Sally's room. He had some experience at this game—though he preferred the clean, manly sport of picking pockets—and he made no noise at all. Signaling to the maid to go on up to bed and leave him to his task, he settled down to wait on the landing until he was certain that Sally was asleep. A silver flask kept watch with him; it had made two journeys to his lips, and come back lighter, before he judged it time to move.

He turned the handle of her door and opened it no more than eighteen inches. Beyond that, Ellen had told him, it squeaked. A gas lamp in the square outside gave sufficient light through the thin curtains for him to be able to see most of the room, and he stood quite still for two minutes, getting his bearings, being particularly careful about the floor; there was nothing worse than a loose edge of carpet or a hastily dropped article of clothing.

The only sound in the room was Sally's quiet breathing. Occasionally the rattle of a late cab came from the road outside, but nothing else was stirring.

Then he moved. He knew where she kept her papers; Ellen had been very free with her information. Hopkins emptied Sally's bag on the carpet, finding it heavier than he expected. And then he found the pistol.

He gaped for a moment, thinking he'd come to the wrong room. But there was Sally, sleeping only four feet away. . . . He picked up the weapon and tested its balance.

"You little beauty," he said to himself. "I'm having you."

It went into his pocket, together with every scrap of paper in sight. Then he stood and looked around. Should he check all the drawers? But they might be full of papers, and what would he do then? After all, of all the bloody stupid things to ask a man to steal, a piece of bloody paper took the bloody biscuit. Now the pistol—that was worth having.

But he wasn't going to kill Sally for it. He looked down at her. *Pretty girl*, he thought; *only a kid. Be a shame when Mrs. Holland catches up with her. But she can arrange her own accidents; I'm not playing that game.*

He left as silently as he'd come, and not a soul heard him go.

BUT HE didn't go far.

As he rounded a dark corner in the wilderness of streets behind Holborn, an arm encircled his neck, a foot swept his legs from under him, and a very heavy knee plummeted into his midriff. It was too sudden; and the knife that slid into his rib cage was cold, very much too cold, and froze his heart at once; and all he had time to think was, *Not the gutter—my new coat—the mud . . .*

Hands ripped the new coat open and plunged into the pockets. A watch and chain; a silver flask; a gold sovereign, and some copper; a diamond pin in the cravat; a few scraps of paper; and what was this? A gun? A voice laughed lightly, and footsteps died away.

And presently it rained. Little scraps of anguish still fluttered in Henry Hopkins's brain; but it was not long before they settled into baffled oblivion as the blood that sustained them leaked away, out of the hole in his breast, and his life mingled with the dirty water in the gutter and then plunged into the sewers and the darkness.

"AH," SAID MRS. REES at breakfast, "our dear guest has descended. And strangely early, for the toast has not yet come. Usually it is all but cold when you arrive. But there is bacon—will you have bacon? And could you contrive to leave it on the plate, unlike the kidneys of yesterday? Though bacon rolls less well than kidneys, I daresay you could force it off the plate if—"

"Aunt Caroline, I have been robbed," said Sally.

Mrs. Rees looked at her with intense and savage surprise.

"I do not understand," she said.

"Someone has come into my bedroom and stolen something. Many things."

"Did you hear that, Ellen?" said Mrs. Rees to the maid, who had just brought in the toast. "Miss Lockhart claims to have been robbed in my house. And does she blame my servants? Do you blame my servants, miss?"

The question was addressed in such a furious tone that Sally nearly quailed.

"I don't know *who* to blame! But when I woke up I found my bag upset all over the floor, and several things missing. And—"

Mrs. Rees had gone red. Sally had never seen anyone so angry; she thought the woman had gone completely insane, and took a step backward in fright.

"See, Ellen, see! She repays our hospitality by pretending to be the victim of a robbery! Tell me, Ellen: was the house broken into? Are there shattered windows, and footprints? Are any other rooms disturbed? Tell me, child. I will not wait a moment for an answer. Tell me at once!"

"No, ma'am," said the maid in a pious whisper, looking everywhere but at Sally. "I promise you, Mrs. Rees. Everything's where it should be, ma'am."

"On your promise at least I may rely, Ellen. Then tell me, miss—" Turning back to Sally, her face now twisted like some tribal mask, pale eyes bulging and papery lips drawn in a sneer, "Tell me why these robbers who did not enter the house should select you for their imaginary attentions? What did *you* have that anyone would want?"

"Some papers," said Sally, who was now shaking from head to foot. She could not understand it: Mrs. Rees seemed possessed.

"Some papers? Some papers? You wretched girl—*papers*—let me see the scene of the crime. Let me see it. No, Ellen, I can rise without assistance. I am not so old that all the world may take advantage of my weakness—out of my way, girl, out of my way!"

The last words came in a shriek to Sally, who, confused, hovered between the table and the door. Ellen, solicitous, stood aside smartly, and Mrs. Rees tottered up the stairs. At the door of Sally's room she stopped, waiting for it to be opened, and again it was Ellen who was there to do it, Ellen who took her arm as she entered, Ellen who cast—for the first time—a look of sly triumph at Sally, who had followed.

Mrs. Rees looked around. The bedclothes were piled untidily; Sally's nightgown trailed half across the floor and half over the end of the bed; and two of her drawers were open, with clothes jammed hastily into them. The pathetic little heap of things beside Sally's bag on the floor—a purse, a coin or two, a handkerchief, a pocket diary—were scarcely noticeable. Sally saw that the case was hopeless before Mrs. Rees said a word.

"Well?" was the word. "Well, miss?"

"I must have been mistaken," said Sally. "I beg your pardon, Aunt Caroline."

She spoke almost demurely, because an idea had just come into her head: something quite new. She stooped to pick up the things from the floor and found herself smiling.

"What are you grinning at, miss? Why are you smiling in that insolent fashion? I will not be smiled at."

Sally said nothing, but began to fold her clothes and put them neatly on the bed.

"What are you doing? Answer me! Answer me at once, you impertinent hussy!"

"I'm going to leave," said Sally.

"What? What did you say?"

"I'm going to leave, Mrs. Rees. I can't stay here anymore—I can't and I won't."

A gasp from the lady, another from the maid—and they stood aside as Sally made purposefully for the door.

"I shall send for my things," she said. "You will have the goodness to send them on when I let you know my new address. Good day."

And she left.

AND FOUND HERSELF, once on the pavement outside, quite at a loss what to do next.

She had burned her boats—she was sure of that. She

could never go back to Mrs. Rees; but where else could she go? She walked on steadily, out of Peveril Square, and passed a news agent's; which gave her an idea. With almost the last of her money—three pennies—she bought a copy of *The Times*, and sat down to read it in a nearby churchyard. There was only one page which interested her, and it was not that which bore advertisements for governesses.

Having penciled some notes in the margin of the paper, she walked briskly to Mr. Temple's chambers in Lincoln's Inn. It was a fine morning, after the incessant drizzle of the night before, and the sun lifted her spirits.

Mr. Temple's clerk admitted her. The lawyer was very busy, very busy indeed, but he might be prevailed upon to see her for five minutes. She was shown into the office; Mr. Temple, bald and lean and brisk, got up to shake her hand.

"How much money have I got, Mr. Temple?" she asked, after they had exchanged greetings.

He reached for a large book and wrote down some figures.

"Four hundred and fifty pounds in two and a half percent Treasury Stock; one hundred and eighty ordinary shares in the London and Southeastern Railway Company; two hundred preference shares in the Royal Mail Steam Navigation Company.... Are you sure that you want to know all this?"

"Everything, please." She was following in the newspaper as he read.

He continued. It was not a long list.

"And the income," he concluded, "is, in round terms—"

"About forty pounds a year," she said.

"How did you know that?"

"I worked it out as you were reading the list."

"Good Lord."

"And I believe I have a measure of control over my money?"

"A great deal. Far too much, in my view. I tried to dissuade your father, but nothing would make him change his mind—so I drew up the will as he told me."

"Then it's a good thing you failed. Mr. Temple, I'd like you to arrange to sell three hundred pounds of the Treasury Stock and buy equally among the following companies: the Great Western Railway Company; the Gas, Light, and Coke Company; and C. H. Parsons, Limited."

His jaw fell, but he wrote down her instructions.

"Furthermore," she said, "those preference shares in the Royal Mail Steam Navigation Company—sell those, please, and buy ordinary shares in the P and O. That should bring the income up to a little over fifty. I shall look at it again in a month or so, when ... when I have time. I take it that there is some money paid on my account now to Mrs. Rees?"

"Mrs. Rees was paid ..." He turned a page. "One hundred pounds on your father's death. That was a legacy, of course, not a payment for any service that might be rendered. The trustees—of whom I am one—came to an agreement by which the income from the trust should be paid on your behalf to Mrs. Rees while you remained under her roof."

"I see," said Sally. That woman had been receiving all her income, while accusing her of living on charity! "Well," she went on, "I have been discussing things with Mrs. Rees, and it will be best if the income is paid directly to me from now on. Could you arrange for it to be paid into my account at the Strand branch of the London and Midland Bank?"

Mr. Temple looked decidedly troubled. He sighed and wrote it down, but said nothing.

"And finally, Mr. Temple, may I have some money now? You didn't mention a current account, but there must be one."

He turned a page in her ledger.

"It contains twenty-one pounds, six shillings, and ninepence," he said. "How much would you like to withdraw?"

"Twenty pounds, please."

He opened a cashbox and counted out the money in gold.

"Miss Lockhart, I ask you simply—is this wise?"

"It is what I want to do. And I have the right to do it, so it will be done. One day, Mr. Temple, I promise I'll tell you why. Oh—there is another thing. . . ."

He pushed the cashbox away and faced her. "Yes?"

"Did my father ever mention a Major Marchbanks?"

"I have heard the name. I don't think your father had seen him for many years. A friend from his army days, I believe."

"Or a Mrs. Holland?"

He shook his head.

"Or anything at all called the Seven Blessings?"

"What an extraordinary name. No, Miss Lockhart, he didn't."

"Then I won't take up any more of your time, Mr. Temple; but what about my father's share of his own firm? I had expected that to be worth something."

He stroked his jaw and looked ill at ease.

"Miss Lockhart, you and I will have to have a talk. Not now—I'm busy—but it'll keep for a week or so. Your father was a very unusual man, and you're a very unusual young lady, if I may say so. You're conducting yourself in a most businesslike way. I'm impressed. So I'll tell you something now that was going to keep till you were a little older: I'm worried about that firm, and I'm worried about what your father did before he left for the East. You're quite right: there should be more money. But the fact is that he sold his share outright, for ten thousand pounds, to his partner, Mr. Selby."

"And where is that money now?"

"That's what I'm worried about. It's vanished."

8

---◆---

The Passions of Art

THERE WERE FEW PLACES, IN THE ENGLAND OF 1872, where a young lady could go on her own to sit, and think, and possibly drink some tea. The tea was not so important yet; but sooner or later she would have to eat, and there was only one class of well-dressed young women who moved freely in and out of hotels and restaurants; and Sally had no desire to be mistaken for one of those.

But she was, as Mr. Temple had said, a very unusual young lady. She wasn't afraid of being alone, for one thing. The independence of mind her father's teaching had given her stood her in good stead; problems, she thought, were things you faced, not things you ran away from.

She left Lincoln's Inn and walked slowly along the river until she found a bench under the statue of some bewigged king, and then she sat down to watch the traffic.

The biggest blow was the loss of her pistol. She had copied the three stolen papers—the message from the East, Major Marchbanks's letter, and the single page from the book—into her diary, so they were preserved. But the pistol had been a gift from her father, and besides, it might one day save her life.

But what she wanted most was to talk. Jim would have been the ideal person to talk to, but it was a Tuesday, and he would be working. Then there was Major March-banks—but Mrs. Holland might be watching the house, as she had before.

Then she remembered the card tucked into her diary. Thank heaven the thief had not removed that!

FREDERICK GARLAND
PHOTOGRAPHIC ARTIST
45, Burton Street
London

She had some money now. She hailed a cab and gave the driver the address.

BURTON STREET was a shabby little place in the neighborhood of the British Museum. The door of number 45 was open; a painted sign proclaimed that W. and F. Garland, Photographers, conducted their business there. Sally went in and found a dusty, narrow shop, crowded with various photographic bits and pieces—magic lanterns, bottles of chemicals, cameras, and the like—standing on the counter and packed untidily on the shelves. There was no one there, but the inner door was open, and Sally could hear voices raised in a violent quarrel. One of them was the photographer's.

"I will not!" he shouted. "I detest all lawyers on principle, and that goes for their spotty little clerks as well—"

"I'm not talking about lawyers, you lazy oaf!" came the equally passionate voice of a young woman. "It's an accountant you need, not a bloody lawyer—and if you don't get something sorted out soon there won't be any business left at all!"

"Balderdash! Stick to your mumming, you shrieking virago—here, Trembler, there's a customer in the shop."

A little wizened man ran anxiously out, with the air of one ducking away from flying bullets. He shut the door behind him, but the shouting continued.

"Yes, miss?" came a nervous voice from behind a huge, soup-strainer mustache.

"I came to see Mr. Garland. But if he's busy . . ."

She looked at the door, and he cowered away from it, as if expecting some missile to come hurtling through.

"You don't want me to go and fetch him, do you, miss?" he pleaded. "I daren't, honest."

"Well . . . no. I suppose not at the moment."

"Was it about a sitting, miss? We can fit you in any-time. . . ."

He was looking at an appointment book.

"No. No, it was—"

The door opened, and the little man ducked under the counter.

"Be damned to the whole tribe of—" came a roar from the photographer, and then he stopped at once. He stood in the doorway and grinned, and Sally realized that she'd forgotten how full of life and movement his face was.

"Hello!" he said, in the friendliest possible manner. "Miss Lockhart, isn't it?"

He was suddenly propelled into the shop, and there in his place stood a young woman two or three years older than Sally. Her red hair flared over her shoulders, her eyes blazed, and she held a sheaf of papers in her clenched fist. Sally thought: *But she's beautiful!* And so she was— astonishingly lovely.

"You're slovenly, Frederick Garland!" she stormed.

"These bills have been waiting since Easter, and what have you done about it? What have you spent the money on? What do you ever do but—"

"What do I do?" He turned back to her, his voice rising powerfully. "What do I do? I work harder than any band of painted mummers who loaf about in the back of a theater! What about the polarizing lens—d'you think I got that by whistling for it? And the gelatin process—"

"The devil take your bloody gelatin process. What do you mean, *loaf*? I will not have my work insulted by a second-rate . . . daguerrotypist whose only idea of art is—"

"Daguerrotypist? Second-rate? How dare you, you ranting puppet—"

"Skulking bankrupt!"

"Howling termagant!"

And the next moment he turned to Sally, as calm as a bishop, and said politely: "Miss Lockhart, may I introduce my sister, Rosa?"

Sally blinked and found herself smiling. The young woman held out her hand and smiled in return. Of course they were brother and sister—he was nowhere near as good-looking as she was, but the sheer life and energy of expression was the same in both of them.

"Have I called at a bad time?" she said.

He laughed, and the little man came out from under the counter like a tortoise out of its shell.

"No," said Miss Garland, "not at all. If you want to be photographed, you've come just in time—there might not be a business at all tomorrow."

She cast an angry glance at her brother, who waved it aside airily.

"No, I don't want to be photographed," said Sally. "In fact, I only came because . . . well, I met Mr. Garland last Friday, and . . ."

"Oh! You're the girl from Swaleness! He told me all about it."

"Can I go back to me plates now?" said the little man.

"Yes, go on, Trembler," said the photographer, seating himself calmly on the counter as the little man touched his brow nervously and scuttled out. "He's preparing some plates, you see, Miss Lockhart, and he got a little worried. My sister tried to assassinate me."

"Someone ought to," Rosa said darkly.

"She's very excitable. She's an actress—can't help it."

"I'm sorry to interrupt," said Sally. "I shouldn't have come."

"Are you in trouble?" said Rosa.

Sally nodded. "But I don't want to—"

"Is it the witch again?" asked the photographer.

"Yes. But . . ." She stopped. *I wonder if I dare?* she thought. "Did you say—I'm sorry, but I couldn't help hearing—did you say you needed an accountant?"

"So my sister tells me."

"Of course we do," Rosa said hotly. "This photographic clown has got us into the most appalling muddle, and if we don't sort it out soon—"

"Exaggeration," he said. "It won't take long to sort out."

"Well, do it then!" she flared at him.

"I can't. I haven't got the time, I haven't got the talent, and I certainly haven't got the inclination."

"I was going to say," Sally went on diffidently, "that I'm good with figures—I used to help my father draw up his company balance sheets, and he taught me all about bookkeeping and accounts—I'd be glad to help! I mean, I came here to ask for—for help. But if I can do something in exchange, that would be better, perhaps. I don't know."

She finished lamely, blushing. That speech had been difficult to make, but she was determined to get through it. She looked down.

"D'you mean it?" said the girl.

"Honestly. I know I'm good with figures, or else I shouldn't have said anything."

"Then we'd be delighted," said Frederick Garland. "You see?" he said to his sister. "I told you there was nothing to worry about. Miss Lockhart, you'll join us for lunch?"

LUNCH, in their bohemian household, consisted of a jug of ale, the remains of a large joint of roast beef, a fruitcake, and a bag of apples, which Rosa said she had been given the night before by one of her admirers, a porter in Covent Garden market. They ate it, with the help of one large pocketknife and their fingers (and empty chemical jars for the beer) at the crowded laboratory bench behind the shop. Sally was enchanted.

"You'll have to forgive 'em, miss, begging yer pardon," said the little man, whose only name seemed to be Trembler. "It ain't want of breedin', it's want of money."

"But think what the rich are missing, Trembler," said Rosa. "Who'd ever discover how delicious beef and plum cake are unless they had nothing else to eat?"

"Oh, come on, Rosa," said Frederick, "we don't starve. We've never gone without a meal. We go without washing dishes, though," he said to Sally. "A matter of principle. No dishes, no washing."

Sally wondered how they managed with soup, but

didn't have time to ask, for every gap in the conversation was filled by their questions, and by the time the meal was over they knew as much as she did about the mystery. Or mysteries.

"Well, Sally, tell me this," said Frederick (somehow, during the consumption of the plum cake, they had progressed to first-name terms without noticing it). "Why don't you go to the police?"

"I don't really know. Or—yes, I do know. It's just that it seems to concern my birth—or my father's life in India—my background, anyway—and I want to keep that to myself till I know more about it."

"Of course you do," said Rosa. "The police are so stupid, Fred—it's the last thing she should do."

"You have been robbed," Frederick pointed out. "Twice."

"I'd still rather not. There are so many reasons . . . I haven't even told the lawyer about being robbed."

"And now you've left home," said Rosa. "Where are you going to live?"

"I don't know. I must find a room."

"Well, that's easy. We've got acres of space. You can have Uncle Webster's room for the time being. Trembler will show you where it is. I've got to go and rehearse now. I'll be back later!"

And before Sally could thank her, she had swept out.

"Are you sure?" said Sally to Frederick.

"Well, of course! And if we're going to be businesslike, you can pay rent for it."

She thought of the tent he'd let her hide in on the seafront, and her foolish offer to pay, and found herself confused; but he was looking away and writing something on a scrap of paper.

"Trembler," he said, "could you run across to Mr. Eeles's and ask to borrow these books?"

"Righto, Mr. Fred. But there's them plates to be got up, and the magnesium."

"Do them when you come back."

The little man left, and Sally said, "Is his name really Trembler?"

"His name is Theophilus Molloy. But honestly, could you call anyone Theophilus? I couldn't. And his previous associates used to call him Trembler; I suppose the name stuck. He's an unsuccessful pickpocket. I met him when he tried to pick mine. He was so relieved when I stopped him that he practically wept with gratitude, and he's been with us ever since. But look—I think you ought to read your newspaper. I see you have a copy of *The Times*. Have a look at page six."

Sally, surprised, did as he said. Near the foot of the page she found a small paragraph which related the same news that Mr. Hopkins's rather brisker paper had told him the day before.

"Major Marchbanks dead?" she said. "I can't believe it. And this man—the one in the checkered suit—he was the one who stole the book! The one in the train! Do you think he'd just come from . . ."

"One of the old girl's agents," Fred said. "Probably skulking around at Swaleness. Mrs. Holland must have got a message to him. And then last night he came back for the rest of it."

"He took my gun as well."

"Naturally he would, seeing it there. But you've got a copy of the papers—let's have a look."

She opened her diary and passed it across the top of the scarred pine bench. He bent over it to read.

" '. . . a place of darkness, under a knotted rope. Three red lights shine on the spot when the moon pulls on the water. Take it. It is clearly yours by my gift, and by the laws of England. *Antequam haec legis . . .*' Good Lord."

"What? Can you read the Latin?"

"Don't you know what it says?"

"No, what is it?"

"It says: 'By the time you read this, I shall be dead. May my memory be . . .'—what's the word—'may I be as swiftly forgotten.' "

She felt suddenly cold. "He knew what was going to happen," she said.

"Perhaps it wasn't murder," said Frederick. "Perhaps it was suicide."

"The poor man," said Sally. "He was so unhappy." She found tears in her eyes. It was the cold, bare house, and the gentle way he'd spoken to her. . . . "I'm sorry," she said.

He shook his head and offered a clean handkerchief. When she had dried her tears, he said, "He's talking about a hiding place, you realize. He's telling you where the ruby is, and saying that it belongs to you."

"By the laws of England," she said. "Which law could make it belong to me? I can't understand."

"Nor can I—yet. And then there's the opium smoker, Mr. Bedwell. In some ways he's easier to deal with. . . . Ah, here's Trembler."

"Here you are, Mr. Fred," said Trembler, coming in with three large books. "Can I do me plates now?"

"By all means—aha—*Crockford's Clerical Directory*. Bedwell—Bedwell . . ."

Frederick flicked through the pages of a fat and solemn-looking volume until he found what he was looking for.

" 'Bedwell, the Reverend Nicholas Armbruster. Born 1842; educated at Rugby and Balliol College, Oxford; graduated B.A., 1861, M.A., 1864; Curate of St. John's, Summertown, Oxford.' "

"They're twins," said Sally.

"Exactly. I should think that if anyone can get this man out of Holland's Lodgings, it'll be his own brother. We'll go to Oxford tomorrow and see him."

DURING THE REST of that day and evening Sally learned a little about the Garland family. He was twenty-one, she eighteen, and the house and shop belonged to their uncle, Webster Garland, who was, according to Frederick, the greatest photographer of the age. He was at present in Egypt, and Frederick was in charge, with the result that had so enraged Rosa. Trembler told her all this while she sat in the back room and began to make sense of the accounts. Frederick went out at three o'clock to take some pictures at the British Museum, and Trembler became loquacious.

"He's an artist, miss, that's the trouble," he said. "There's plenty of money in the photography game for them as wants to make it, but Mr. Fred ain't interested in yer portraits and yer weddings. I've seen him spend a whole week sitting as still as stone in one spot, waiting for the right light on a patch o' water. He's good, mind you. But he will invent things, and it swallows the money at a rate you wouldn't believe. It's Miss Rosa what keeps this place afloat."

Rosa was an actress, as Frederick had said, at present

playing in *Dead or Alive* at the Queen's Theater. Only a tiny part, said Trembler, but she was bound to be a star one day. With those looks, and that temperament—well, the world had no chance of resisting her. But so far the rewards were meager, though her income was the greater part of the revenue of 45 Burton Street.

"But Frederick's made quite a lot of money," said Sally, sorting through a pile of untidy receipts and scribbled bills and putting income on one side, expenditure on the other. "In fact, there's quite a lot of money coming in. But it all seems to go out again."

"If you can see a way of keeping some of that cash in, miss, you'll be doing 'em the greatest favor as could be done. For he'll never manage it."

She worked on through the afternoon, gradually reducing the chaos of unpaid bills and tattered invoices to some sort of order. She enjoyed it immensely. Here at last was something she understood and could deal with, something with a clear and straightforward meaning! Trembler brought her a cup of tea at five, and from time to time left the back room to serve a customer in the shop.

"What do you sell most of?" Sally asked.

"Photographic plates and chemicals. He laid in a great store of stereoscopes, Mr. Fred, a few months back, when he got some money for an invention. But they ain't selling. People want the pictures to go with 'em, and he's hardly got any of them."

"He ought to take some."

"You tell him, then. I've tried, but he won't listen to me."

"What sort do people like best?"

"Views is best. Stereoscopic views is different from ordinary ones. Then there's humorous, sentimental, romantic, devotional, and risky. Oh, and temperance. But he won't touch 'em. Says they're vulgar."

By the time Frederick came back, at six o'clock, she had begun to make out a complete statement of their accounts, setting out precisely what they had earned and spent in the six months since Webster Garland had gone to Egypt.

"*Formidable!*" he said cheerfully, setting down his camera and darkroom tent before shutting the shop door.

"It'll take another day or so to get it completely straight," she said. "And you'll have to tell me what some of these notes say. Is it your writing?"

" 'Fraid it is. What does the whole thing look like? Good or bad? Am I bankrupt?"

"You must press to have your bills paid on time. There's fifty-six pounds seven shillings owed to you from months ago, and twenty guineas from last month. If you get that in, you can pay most of what you owe. But you must do it properly and keep proper records."

"No time."

"You must make time. It's important."

"Too boring."

"Then pay someone to do it for you. It's got to be done, or you *will* be bankrupt. You don't need more money— you just need to manage what you've got. And I think I can find some ways of making more, in any case."

"Would you like the job?"

"Me?"

He was looking at her quite seriously. His eyes were green; she hadn't noticed that before.

"Why not?" he said.

"I—I don't know," she said. "I've done this today because . . . Well, it needed to be done. In exchange for your helping me to sort out . . . But I mean you need a professional adviser. Someone who could, I don't know, sort of take charge of the business side altogether . . ."

"Well, do you want to do it?"

She shook her head, and then shrugged, and found herself nodding, and then shrugged again quickly. He laughed, and she blushed.

"Look," he said, "it seems to me that you're just the person for the job. You're going to have to get some sort of situation, after all. You can't live on a tiny income. . . . And do you want to be a governess?"

She shuddered. "No!"

"Or a nursemaid or a cook or something? Of course not. And you can do this, and you seem to be good at it."

"I love doing it."

"Well, why do you hesitate?"

"All right. I will—I'll do it. And thank you."

They shook hands and agreed to terms. She was to be paid at first by being given her board and lodging free; there was no money to pay her a wage until they earned some, as she pointed out. When the firm was making money, she would be paid fifteen shillings a week.

Once that was settled, Sally felt a glow of happiness; and to celebrate their agreement, Frederick sent out for a hot meat pie from the chophouse around the corner. They cut it into four, saving a piece for Rosa, and sat around the laboratory bench to eat it. Trembler made some coffee, and as she drank it Sally found herself wondering what it was that was so unusual about this household. There was something deeper than not washing dishes, than eating off a laboratory bench at odd hours. She puzzled over it as she sat in a sagging old armchair beside the fire in the kitchen, with Trembler reading the paper at the table and Frederick whistling softly as he did something with some chemicals in a corner. She still hadn't found the answer when, much later, Rosa came in, cold and noisy and triumphantly bearing a large pineapple, and woke up Sally (she having inadvertently fallen asleep) and stormed at the others for not showing her to her room. She was still puzzling when she climbed shivering into the narrow little bed and pulled the blankets up around her; but just before she fell asleep, she saw the answer. *Of course!* she thought. *They don't think of Trembler as a servant. And they don't think of me as a girl. We're all equal. That's what's so odd. . . .*

9

A Journey to Oxford

MRS. HOLLAND LEARNED OF THE DEATH OF HENRY HOP-kins from one of her cronies, a woman who performed some dingy function in the workhouse of St. George's, a street or two away. This woman had heard it from a factory girl in her lodgings, whose brother was a crossing-sweeper who worked the same street as a news vendor whose cousin had spoken to the man who'd found the body; and in that way the news of criminal London spread from one place to another. Mrs. Holland was nearly speechless with rage at Hopkins's incompetence. To let himself be killed in that tame fashion! Of course, the police would never trace the killer; but Mrs. Holland intended to. The word went out, filtering like smoke through the alleys and courts, the streets and wharves and docksides: Mrs. Holland at Hangman's Wharf would give a good deal to know who'd killed Henry Hopkins. She sent out the word and waited. Something would turn up, and it wouldn't take long.

THERE WAS one citizen who felt pursued by Mrs. Holland already, and that was Samuel Selby, shipping agent, Sally's father's ex-partner.

Her letter took him completely by surprise. He had thought that blackmail was impossible: the tracks had been well covered. And from Wapping, of all places. . . .

But after a day or so spent in quiet panic, he thought again.

There were things in this letter that no one should have known about, true. But there were more incriminating things that weren't even mentioned; and where was the proof? Where were the invoices, the bills of lading, the ships' papers that would sink him? There wasn't a hint of them.

No, he thought, *perhaps there's less to this than there seems. But I'd better make sure. . . .*

Accordingly, he wrote a letter:

> Samuel Selby
> Shipping Agent
> Cheapside
> Tuesday 29 October 1872

Mrs. M. Holland
Holland's Lodgings
Hangman's Wharf
Wapping

Dear Mrs. Holland,

Thank you for your communication of the 25th inst. I beg to inform you that your client's proposal is not without interest, and I would like to invite your client to meet me at my office at 10 o'clock on the morning of Thursday 31st.

> I beg to remain,
> Your humble servant,
> S. Selby

There, he thought as he posted it; *we'll see what that brings.* He was inclined to doubt the existence of this client, this mysterious gentleman, altogether; dockside gossip, more like. Nothing more than that.

WEDNESDAY MORNING was cold, with a mist in the air. Frederick announced to Sally at breakfast (boiled eggs, cooked in the kettle) that he would go to Oxford with her. He could always take some photographs, he said—and besides, she might need someone to keep her awake on the train. He spoke lightly, but she knew he meant she was in danger; without her gun she felt vulnerable, and was glad of his company.

The journey passed quickly. They were in Oxford by midday and had lunch at the Railway Hotel. Sally had talked easily on the train—talking to Frederick, and listening to him, seemed the most natural and agreeable thing in the world—but once seated facing him across a table set with cutlery and napkins and glasses, she found herself absurdly tongue-tied.

"What are you scowling for?" he said at one point.

She had been staring down at her plate, trying to think of something to say. And now she blushed. "I wasn't scowling," she said, sounding petulant and childish—and realizing it. He raised his eyebrows and said nothing more.

The meal was not a success, in short, and they parted immediately afterward, she to take a cab to St. John's Vicarage, and he to photograph some buildings.

"Go carefully," he said as she left, and she wanted to go back and explain her silence at lunch, but it was too late.

The vicarage at St. John's was about two miles from the center of Oxford, in the village of Summertown. The cab took her up the Banbury Road, past the newly built large brick villas of North Oxford. The vicarage was next to the church in a quiet little road overhung with elm trees.

The mist of the morning had cleared now, and a watery sun was shining faintly as Sally knocked at the door.

"The vicar's away, but Mr. Bedwell's in, miss," said the maid who opened the door to her. "Through here, if you please, in the study. . . ."

The Reverend Nicholas Bedwell was a stocky, fair-haired man with a humorous expression. His eyes widened as she came in, and she saw with surprise that his look was one of admiration. He offered her a chair and turned his own away from the desk to face her.

"Well, Miss Lockhart?" he said jovially. "What can I do for you? Banns of a marriage?"

"I think I have some news of your brother," she said.

He leaped to his feet, and a sudden excitement flooded his face.

"I knew it!" he cried, smacking his fist into his palm. "He's alive? Matthew's alive?"

She nodded.

"Tell me!" he said, his blue eyes blazing. "Tell me all you know!"

"He's in a lodging house in Wapping. He's been there about a week or ten days, I suppose, and . . . he's smoking opium. I don't think he can get away."

The curate's face darkened at once, and he sank into his chair. Sally told him briefly of how she'd come to hear about it, and he listened intently, shaking his head as she finished.

"Two months ago I had a telegram," he said. "They told me he was dead, that his ship had gone down. The schooner *Lavinia*—he was the second mate."

"My father was on board," said Sally.

"Oh, my dear young lady!" he exclaimed. "They said there were no survivors."

"He drowned."

"I'm so sorry. . . ."

"But you say you knew your brother was alive?"

"We're twins, Miss Lockhart. All our lives we've each felt the other's emotions, known what the other was doing—and I was sure he wasn't dead. I was as certain of it as I am of this chair!" He banged the arm of the chair he sat in. "No doubt at all! But of course I didn't know where he was. You mentioned opium . . ."

"That's probably why he can't get away."

"That drug is the invention of the devil. It's ruined more lives, wasted more fortunes, and poisoned more bodies than even alcohol. There are times, you know, when I'd willingly leave this parish and everything I've worked for, and spend my life fighting against it. . . . My brother became a slave to it three years ago, in the East. I—I felt that, too. And unless it's stopped—unless he's stopped—it'll kill him in the end."

Sally was silent. The curate was staring fiercely into the cold fireplace, as if the ashes that lay there were those of the drug itself. His fists were clenching and unclenching slowly; Sally noticed that they were large, and hard, and thoroughly formidable. There was a certain battered quality about his face, too—his cheek was scarred, and his nose slightly flattened. Apart from the clothes he wore, he was most unclergyman-like.

"But you see," she said after a moment, "your brother knows something about my father's death. He must. The little girl said he had a message for me."

He looked up suddenly. "Of course. I'm sorry—this concerns you, too, doesn't it? Well now—to business. We must get him out of that place as soon as possible. I can't leave the parish today or tomorrow—evensong this evening, and a funeral tomorrow . . ." He was leafing through a diary. "Friday's clear. Well, it isn't, but nothing I can't put off. There's a man at Balliol who'll take a service for me. We'll get Matthew out of there on Friday."

"But what about Mrs. Holland?"

"What about her?"

"Adelaide said she's keeping him prisoner. And—"

"It's the opium that's keeping him prisoner. This is England! You can't hold people against their will."

His expression was so pugnacious that Sally feared for anyone who tried to stop him.

"There's one thing, though," he went on more calmly. "He'll need some of that filthy drug to keep him going. I'll bring him back here and get him straight again, but without the drug he'll never manage. I'll have to wean him off it bit by bit. . . ."

"How will you get him out?"

"With my fists, if necessary. He'll come. But . . . look, could you do something for me? Could you find me some of the drug?"

"I could try. Of course I will. But wouldn't they sell it in Oxford? At a pharmacist's?"

"Only in the form of laudanum. And the smoker needs the gum, or the resin, or whatever the evil stuff is. I hesitate to ask, but . . . if you can't, we'll have to do without."

"I can certainly try," she said.

He put his hand in his pocket and drew out three sovereigns.

"Take this. Buy as much as you can. And if Matthew doesn't need it after all, then at least it's out of the hands of some other wretch."

He came to the door with her and shook her hand.

"Thank you for coming," he said. "It's a great relief to know where he is. I'll come to your rooms at Burton Street on Friday, then. Expect me around noon."

SALLY WALKED back into Oxford to save the cab fare. The road was broad and pleasant, and busy with carts and carriages; these quiet houses and leafy gardens seemed to be on a different planet from the darkness and mystery and sudden death she was returning to. She passed one house where three young children, the eldest not much younger than she was, were building a bonfire in a cheerful, untidy garden. Their shouts and laughter made her feel cold and deprived; where had her childhood gone? And yet only an hour or two earlier she had felt on fire with embarrassment because she was a child and had none of the ease of an adult. She would have given anything to be able to forget London and Mrs. Holland and the Seven Blessings, and to live in one of these large, comfortable houses, with children and animals and bonfires and lessons and games.... Perhaps even now it wasn't too late to become a governess, or a nurse, or ...

But it was. Her father had died, and something was wrong, and there was no one but herself to set it right. She quickened her pace and entered the broad road of St. Giles that led to the center of the city.

There was another hour and a half before she was going to meet Frederick. She spent it looking around the city— aimlessly at first, since the old college buildings held little interest for her. But then she saw a photographer's shop and made for it at once. She spent an hour talking to the proprietor and looking at his stock, and came away much enlightened and much happier, having entirely forgotten (for a little while at least) Wapping, and opium, and the ruby.

"I KNEW I was right, to come to Oxford," said Fredrick in the train. "You'll never guess who I've been talking to this afternoon."

"Tell me, then," said Sally.

"Well, I went to see an old school friend of mine at New College. And he introduced me to a chap called Chandra Sen—an Indian. He comes from Agrapur."

"Really?"

"He's a mathematician. Very scientific, very austere. But we talked about cricket for a bit, and he loosened up, and I asked him what he knew about the Ruby of Agrapur. He was astounded. Apparently there are more stories about that stone than just about any other piece of rock in India. And no one's seen it since the mutiny. The maharajah was murdered, you know."

"When? By whom?"

"It was during that time, evidently, because his body was discovered after the relief of Lucknow. But no one knows who did it. And the ruby was missing, and it's never turned up since. But there was such confusion at that time and so much death and destruction. . . . He asked me how I'd heard of it, and I said I'd read something in an old book of travel. Then he told me something very odd. He didn't believe in this himself—far too rational—but there was a legend that the evil of the stone would persist until it was laid to rest by a woman who was its equal. I asked him what that meant, and he said rather sniffily that he had no idea, it was just superstition. Nice chap, but rather prim. Still, we've learned something, even if we don't know what it means."

She nodded, and they fell silent for a while.

Then he said: "And what have you been finding out? You said at the station you had something to tell me."

With an effort she tugged her mind away from India.

"Stereographic pictures," she said. "I spent an hour or so in a photographer's shop. Do you know how many people came into the place while I was there and bought stereographic pictures? Six of them, in just one hour. D'you know how many have come into your shop and asked for them?"

"I haven't the vaguest idea."

"Trembler says more people ask for them than for anything else. And why buy all those stereoscopes if you don't sell the pictures to go in them?"

"But we sell stereographic cameras. People can take the pictures for themselves."

"They don't want to. Taking stereographs is a job for an expert. And anyway, people like pictures of far-off countries and things like that—things they can't see for themselves."

"But—"

"People could buy them just as they buy books and magazines. They'd buy thousands! What sort of pictures did you take today?"

"I was trying a new Voigtlander two-hundred-millimeter lens with a variable diaphragm I'm trying to get right."

"But what sort of pictures?"

"Oh, buildings and things."

"Well, you could take stereographs of places like Oxford and Cambridge and sell them as a set. 'The Colleges of Oxford'—or 'The Bridges of London'—or 'Famous Castles.' Honestly, Frederick, you could sell thousands."

He was scratching his head; his tow-colored hair stood up stiffly, and his face, in the mobile, vivid way he shared with his sister, seemed to be struggling to contain three or four different expressions at once.

"I don't know," he said. "I could take them easily enough—it's no more difficult than taking an ordinary photograph. But I couldn't sell them."

"I could, though."

"Ah, well, that's different. But photography's changing, you know. In a few years' time we won't be using these great clumsy glass plates at all. We'll be taking negatives on paper in lightweight cameras. We'll be working at phenomenal speeds. There's all kinds of work going on. . . . Well, I'm doing some of it myself. And no one will look at old-fashioned stereographs then."

"But I'm talking about *now*. At the moment people want them, and they'll pay you for them. And how can you do anything exciting in the future if you don't make some money now?"

"Well, you could be right. Got any more ideas?"

"Lots. Display the goods differently, for a start. And advertise. And—"

She stopped and gazed out the window. The train was steaming along beside the Thames; the late autumn afternoon was closing in rapidly, and the river looked gray and cold. *This water will be flowing past Hangman's Wharf soon*, she thought. *We're both going that way.*

"What is it?" he said.

"Frederick, can you help me buy some opium?"

10

Madame Chang

NEXT AFTERNOON, FREDERICK TOOK SALLY TO THE East End.

The year before, he had helped his uncle in a project to photograph scenes of London life, using an experimental magnesium light. The light had only been partly successful, but Frederick had made a number of acquaintances in the course of the project, including the proprietress of a Limehouse opium den: a lady by the name of Madame Chang.

"Most of these places are abominable," he said as they sat in the omnibus. "A shelf to lie on, a filthy blanket, and a pipe, and that's all. But Madame Chang takes care of her customers and keeps the place clean. I suppose the reason is that she doesn't take the stuff herself."

"Are they always Chinese? Why doesn't the government stop them?"

"Because the government grows the stuff itself, and sells it, and makes a handsome profit."

"Surely not!"

"Don't you know anything of history?"

"Well—no."

"We fought a war with China thirty years ago over opium. The Chinese objected to English merchants smuggling opium into the country and tried to ban it; so we went to war and forced them to take it. They grow it in India, you see, under government supervision."

"But that's horrible! And our government's still doing that now? I don't believe it."

"You'd better ask Madame Chang. Time to get out now; we'll walk the rest of the way."

The omnibus had stopped at the West India Dock Station. Beyond the gate into the dock, a line of warehouses stretched for over half a mile to the left, and above their roofs the masts of ships and the jibs of cranes pointed to the gray sky like skeletal fingers.

They set off to the right, toward the river. They passed the large square dock offices, where she supposed her father must have come many times on business, and then turned down an alley and into a maze of courts and side streets. Some of them were not even named, but Frederick knew the way and never hesitated. Barefoot children, ragged and filthy, played among the rubbish and the streams of stinking water that trickled thickly over the cobbles. Women standing in their doorways fell silent as the two passed, and stared with hostile eyes, arms folded, until they had gone by. *They look so old*, thought Sally. Even the children had pinched, old-men's faces, with wrinkled brows and tight-drawn lips. Once they came on a group of men at the entrance to a narrow court. Some were leaning on the wall, some squatting on doorsteps. Their clothes were torn and clotted with dirt, their eyes were full of hatred; one of them stood up and two others shifted away from the wall as Frederick and Sally approached, as if to challenge their right to pass. But Frederick did not change his pace. He walked straight up to the entrance, and the men drew aside at the last moment, looking away.

"Unemployed, poor fellows," said Frederick when they'd turned the corner. "It's either the street corner or the workhouse, and who'd choose the workhouse?"

"But there must be jobs on the ships, or at the docks, or something. People always want workers, don't they?"

"No, they don't. You know, Sally, there are things in London that make opium look no more harmful than tea."

She supposed he meant poverty, and as she looked around she had to agree.

Presently they came to a low wooden door set in the wall of a grimy alley. There was a sign beside the doorway, with some Chinese characters painted in black on red. Frederick tugged the bell handle, and after a minute the door was opened by an old Chinaman. He was dressed in a loose black silk robe, and he had a skullcap and a pigtail. He bowed to them and stood aside as they entered.

Sally looked around. They were in a hall lined with delicately painted wallpaper; all the wood was lacquered in a deep, lustrous red, and an ornate lantern hung from the ceiling. There was a close, sweet smell in the air.

The servant left, to come back after a moment with a middle-aged Chinese woman in a richly embroidered robe. Her hair was severely pinned back, and she had black silk trousers under the robe, and red slippers on her tiny feet. She bowed and gestured toward an inner room.

"Please consent to enter my poor place of business," she said. Her voice was low and musical, and quite without any accent. "You, sir, are Mr. Frederick Garland, the photographic artist. But I have not been honored with the acquaintance of your beautiful companion."

They entered the room. While Frederick explained who Sally was and what they wanted, Sally looked around in wonder. The light was very dim; only two or three Chinese lanterns penetrated the smoky darkness. Everything that could be painted or lacquered in the room was the same deep blood red, and the doorposts and ceiling beams were carved with curling, snarling dragons painted in gold. It gave her a sense of oppressive richness; it seemed as if the room had taken on the shape of the collective dreams of all those who had ever gone there to seek oblivion. At intervals along the walls—it was a large, long room—were low couches, and on each of them was lying a man, apparently asleep. But no! There was a woman hardly older than Sally herself, and another, in middle age; respectably dressed, too. And then one of the sleepers stirred, and the old servant hastened up with a long pipe and knelt on the floor to prepare it.

Frederick and Madame Chang were speaking in low voices behind her, discussing the price of opium and how much Mr. Bedwell might need. Sally looked for somewhere to sit; she felt dizzy. The smoke from the newly lit pipe drifted up to her, sweet and enticing and curious. She breathed in once, and then again, and . . .

Darkness suddenly. Stifling heat.

She was in the Nightmare.

She found herself lying still, with her eyes wide open, searching the darkness. An enormous convulsive fear was squeezing her heart. She tried to move, but could not—and yet it didn't feel as if she were bound; her limbs were too weak to move.

And she knew that only a moment earlier, she'd been awake. . . .

But she was so afraid. The fear grew and grew. It was

worse than ever this time, because it was so much clearer. She knew that any second, close to her in the darkness, a man would begin to scream, and she began to cry in pure fear of it. And then it started.

The scream ripped through the darkness like a sharp sword. She thought she would die from fear. But voices were speaking! This was new—and they were not speaking in English—and yet she could understand them—

"Where is it?"

"Not with me! I pray—I beg of you—it is with a friend—"

"They are coming! Be quick!"

And then a hideous sound, the sound of a sharp instrument sinking into meat—a sort of tearing sound, followed by a sudden gasp and groan as if all the breath had been forced out of a man's lungs at once: and then a gushing, splashing sound that quickly died away into a trickle.

Light.

There was a tiny spark of light somewhere.

(Oh, but she was awake, in the opium den! This was impossible—)

And she could not escape from the dream. It unwound ceaselessly, and she had to live through it. She knew what was coming next: a guttering candle, a man's voice—

"Look! Look at him! My God—"

It was the voice of Major Marchbanks!

This was the point where she had always woken up before—but now something else happened. The light came closer and was held out to one side, and the face of a young man looked down at her: fierce, darkly mustached, with glittering eyes and a trickle of blood down his cheek.

All at once she was awash with fear. She was almost

mad with it. She thought, *I'm going to die—no one can be afraid like this and not die or go mad. . . .*

There was a sharp blow on her cheek. She heard the sound of it a second later; things were out of joint, and everything was dark again. She felt a desolating sense of loss—

And then she was awake, on her knees, her face streaming with tears. Frederick was kneeling beside her, and without thinking she flung her arms around his neck and sobbed. He held her tightly and said nothing. They were in the hall—when had she moved out there? Madame Chang stood a little way off, watching closely.

When she saw that Sally was conscious again, the Chinese woman stepped forward and bowed.

"Please sit here on the divan, Miss Lockhart. Li Ching will bring some refreshment."

She clapped her hands. Frederick helped her onto the silk-covered divan, and the old servant offered her a little porcelain cup containing some hot fragrant drink. She sipped it and felt her head clearing.

"What happened? How long was I—"

"You were affected by the smoke," said Frederick. "You must have inhaled more than you thought. But to go under all at once like that—isn't that very unusual, Madame Chang?"

"This is not her first encounter with the smoke," said the lady, still standing motionless in the gloom.

"I've never smoked opium in my life!" said Sally.

"It distresses me to contradict you, Miss Lockhart. But you have breathed the smoke before. I have seen ten thousand who have taken the smoke, and I know. What did you see in your vision?"

"A scene that—that's come to me many times. A nightmare. A man is being killed and . . . and two other men come along and . . . What can it be, Madame Chang? Am I going mad?"

She shook her head.

"The power of the smoke is unbounded. It hides secrets of the past so well that the sharpest eyes in the brightest daylight would never find them; and then it reveals them all like buried treasure when they have been forgotten. What you saw is a memory, Miss Lockhart, not a dream."

"How can you be sure it's not a fantasy?" said Frederick. "Do you really mean to say that Sally's been under the influence of opium before, and that this nightmare of hers is a memory of the time when it happened? Isn't it possible that it's no more than a dream?"

"It is possible, Mr. Garland. But it is not what happened. I can see plainly what is invisible to you, just as a doctor can see plainly what is troubling his patient. There are a hundred and one signs by which these things may be read, but if you cannot read them, you will see nothing."

Her still figure spoke out of the gloom like the priestess of some ancient cult, full of authority and wisdom. Sally felt the urge to weep again.

She stood up.

"Thank you for explaining, Madame Chang," she said. "Am I . . . am I in danger from the drug? Now that I've taken it once, will I crave to take it again?"

"You have taken it twice, Miss Lockhart," said the lady. "If you are in danger, it is not from the drug. But you have the smoke in your nature now. It has revealed something you did not know; maybe you will crave the smoke not for its own sake, but for the sake of what it can show you."

She bowed, and Frederick, having paid for the opium, stood up to leave. Sally, who still felt dizzy, took the arm he offered, and after exchanging farewells, they left.

Outside it was nearly dark. The cold air was welcome to Sally, who breathed it in gratefully and soon found the pounding in her head diminish a little. Before long, they were in the Commercial Road, and the bustle of traffic, the gaslights, the glowing shop windows, made the opium den seem like a dream itself. But she still trembled, and her sides and back were wet with perspiration.

"Tell me about it," said Frederick.

He hadn't spoken since they left the place; he seemed to know when she wanted silence. *I can trust him*, she thought. So she told it all.

"But Frederick, the worst thing was . . ." She faltered.

"It's all right. You're safe now. But what was the worst thing?"

"The man who spoke—I've heard his voice in my dreams so many times. But this time I recognized it. It was Major Marchbanks; and the other man who looked down at me—Frederick, *he was my father!* What is it all about? What can it mean?"

11

The Stereographic Repertory Company

WHEN THEY RETURNED FROM LIMEHOUSE, SALLY WENT straight to bed and slept dreamlessly for a long time.

She awoke just after dawn. The sky was clear and blue; all the horrors of opium and murder seemed to have vanished with the night, and she felt lighthearted and confident.

Having dressed quickly and lit the kitchen fire, she decided to look over the rest of the house. Rosa herself had suggested this the morning before: they were wasting space, she thought. Perhaps there was room for a lodger.

Sally thought that she was right. The house was much more extensive than it seemed from the street. There were three floors, together with an attic and a cellar, and a long yard behind the house. Two of the rooms were full of photographic apparatus, besides the darkroom and the laboratory. The room beside the shop, on the ground floor, was fitted out as a studio for formal portraits. One of the upstairs rooms was filled with such a miscellaneous collection of things that Sally thought she had stumbled into a museum; but there were two empty attic rooms, and three others which would make very comfortable bedrooms, once decently furnished.

The result of this exploring was revealed to the rest of the household at breakfast. She cooked it: porridge, this time, and very good, too, she thought.

"Frederick, are you busy this morning?" she asked.

"Inordinately. But it can wait."

"Rosa, do you have to rehearse?"

"Not till one. Why?"

"And Trembler, can you spare some time?"

"I dunno, miss. I got some processing to do."

"Well, it won't take long. I just want to tell you how to make some money."

"Well, for that," said Rosa, "you can have all the time you like. How do we do it?"

"It's something I thought about in Oxford the other day. I started to tell Frederick on the train."

"Mmm," he said. "Stereoscopes."

"Not the stereoscopes themselves, but the pictures for them. People are always wanting them. I looked at the rest of the house this morning, and I suddenly realized the kind of thing we could do. There's a room that's full of strange things—spears and drums and idols and I don't know what—"

"Uncle Webster's Cabinet," said Rosa. "He's been collecting it for years."

"So that's one part of it," Sally went on. "The other is Rosa. Wouldn't it be possible to tell a story in pictures? With people—actors—in dramatic situations, like a play—with scenery and things?"

There was a little silence.

"D'you think they'd sell?" said Rosa.

"They'd sell like bleedin' hotcakes," said Trembler. "Give me a thousand, and I'll sell 'em before dinner. Course they'd sell."

"Advertising," said Sally. "We'd take a column in all the papers. Think of a clever name for them. I'd see to all that—that's easy. But what about making them?"

"Nothing to it," said Rosa. "It's a marvelous idea! You could take scenes from popular plays—"

"And sell them to the theater!" said Sally.

"Songs," said Trembler. "Pictures to illustrate all the new songs at the music halls."

"With advertisements on the back," said Sally, "so we get paid extra for each one sold."

"Sally, it's a brilliant idea!" said Rosa. "And with all those props—"

"And there's space outside to set up a real studio. Like an artist's. With room for scenery and sets and all kinds of things."

They all looked at Frederick, who had not spoken. His expression was resigned. He spread his hands wide.

"What can I do?" he said. "Art, farewell!"

"Oh, don't be silly," said Rosa. "Make an art out of this."

He turned and looked at her. Sally thought, *They're like panthers, both of them. They're so alive and intense. . . .*

"You're right!" he said suddenly, and banged the table.

"I don't believe it," said Rosa.

"Of course she's right, you foolish woman. I saw it at once. And we'll do it. But what about the debts?"

"First, no one's actually pressing for money. We owe quite a lot, but if we can show that we're making an effort to pay, I think it'll be all right. Second, there are the accounts which are owing to us. I'm going to send off reminders this morning. And third, Rosa said something about lodgers. You've got room to spare, even with me here. That'll bring in a steady income, even if it's only a few shillings a week. And lastly, there's the stock. Frederick, I want you to go through it with me this morning and we'll get rid of anything that's the slightest bit out-of-date or unnecessary. Have a sale. That'll raise some cash straight away, to pay for the advertisements. Trembler, could you get started on the yard? We need a good clear space. And Rosa—"

She became aware that they were all looking at her with some astonishment. Then Frederick smiled, and she felt a blush burning her cheeks. She looked down, confused.

"I'm sorry! I didn't mean to order you about. . . . I thought—I don't know what I thought. I'm sorry."

"Nonsense! This is what we want!" said Frederick. "We need a manager. That's what you are."

"I'll go and get on," said Trembler, leaving the table.

"And I'll wash the dishes," said Frederick. "Just this once."

He gathered them up and left.

Rosa said, "You know, you're two quite different people."

"Am I?"

"When you're taking charge you're so strong—"

"Me?"

"And when you're not you're so quiet you hardly seem to be there."

"How awful. Am I very bossy? I don't mean to be."

"No! I don't mean that at all. It's just that you seem to know just what to do, and neither Fred nor I have any idea. . . . It's marvelous."

"Rosa, I know so little! I don't know how to talk to people. And what I do know is so . . . I don't know how to put it. It's just not the sort of things that girls know. I love doing this, I can't tell you how much I love it, but it's not normal . . . is it?"

Rosa laughed. She was magnificent; the sunlight seemed to break over her hair like surf over a rock, shattering into thousands of glowing fragments.

"Normal!" she said. "What d'you think I am? An actress—little better than a streetwalker! My parents threw me out because of what I wanted to do. And I've never been so happy—just like you."

"They threw you out? But what about Frederick and your uncle?"

"Fred had an awful row with them. They wanted him to go to university and all that sort of thing. My father's a bishop. It was horrid. Uncle Webster's a sort of old reprobate anyway—they don't acknowledge him. But he doesn't care a bit. Fred's been working with him for three years. He's a genius. They both are. Sally, if you're good at something, you must do it."

"Right!"

Rosa jumped up. "Let's go and sort out those props. I haven't looked in there for ages. . . ."

THEY WORKED all morning, and Trembler, fired by the general enthusiasm, sold a stereoscope to a customer who had only called to book a portrait sitting. Finally, at twelve o'clock, the Reverend Bedwell arrived.

Sally was behind the counter at the time, writing reminders to people who owed them money. She looked up to see the stocky figure of the curate of St. John's and at first didn't recognize him, for he was dressed in a rough old tweed coat and corduroy trousers, without a clerical collar. In fact, he didn't have a collar at all, and he hadn't shaved; so complete was the transformation from mild curate to sullen ruffian that Sally was almost prompted to ask him to act in a stereographic play.

"I do beg your pardon," he said. "Hardly the right sort of clothes to pay a call in. My parson's garb is in a portmanteau in the left luggage office at Paddington. I only hope I can find an empty compartment on the way back—I can hardly return to the vicarage like this...."

Rosa came in and was introduced, and promptly invited him to stay for lunch. He took one look at her and accepted at once. Soon they were all seated, and while they ate the bread and cheese and soup Rosa had set out, he explained what he intended to do.

"I shall take a cab to Hangman's Wharf and drag him out by the collar. He won't resist, but Mrs. Holland might.... Anyway, I'll bring him here, if I may, so that Miss Lockhart can learn what he has to say, and then we'll go back to Oxford."

"I'll come with you," said Sally.

"No, you won't," he said. "He's in danger, and so would you be if you went anywhere near that woman."

"I'll come," said Frederick.

"Splendid. Have you ever boxed?"

"No, but I used to fence at school. Are you expecting a fight?"

"That's why I'm dressed like this. Embarrassing to

start swinging your fists if you're a man of the cloth. The
fact is, I don't know what to expect."

"There's a cutlass in the Cabinet," said Rosa. "D'you
want to take that? And perhaps I ought to make you up as
a pirate, Fred. A patch over one eye, and thick black
whiskers—and then we could stereo-ize you both."

"I'll go as I am," said Frederick. "If I want whiskers, I'll
grow them."

"Is your brother really identical?" said Rosa. "I've met
some identical twins, but they were terribly disappoint-
ing."

"Utterly indistinguishable, Miss Garland. Apart from
the opium—and who knows? If I'd been tempted in that
way, I might have fallen as he did. But what's the time?
We must be going. Thank you for the luncheon. We'll be
back . . . sometime later!"

He left with Frederick, and Rosa sat thoughtfully for a
minute.

"Identical twins," she said. "What an opportunity . . .
Good grief! Is that really the time? I'll be late—Mr. Toole
will be furious . . ."

Mr. Toole was the actor-manager she was rehearsing
with, and apparently a stickler for all kinds of rules. She
threw on her cloak and left quickly.

Trembler went back to the yard, leaving Sally on her
own. The house was suddenly quiet and empty. Mr. Bedwell had left a newspaper, and she picked it up intending
to look at the advertisements. She saw that a firm called
the London Stereographic Company was offering for sale
newly taken portraits of Mr. Stanley, the famous explorer,
and the latest portrait of Dr. Livingstone. There were several other subjects for sale; but no one had thought of dra-

matic scenes or stories in pictures. They would have the market to themselves.

Then her eye was caught by a little advertisement in the personal column:

DISAPPEARED. Missing, since Tuesday 29 October, a YOUNG LADY, aged 16; slender, with fair hair and brown eyes; wore either a black muslin dress and black cloak, or a dark green holland dress, shoes with brass buckles. Took with her a small leather traveling bag, initials V.L. Any information will be thankfully received by Mr. Temple of Temple and King, Lincoln's Inn.

Sally suddenly felt cold, and very visible, as if the whole population of London were looking for her. She must get some different clothes! And stay inside as much as possible. Though she couldn't keep out of sight forever ... surely London was big enough to hide in ...

The trouble was, she just didn't know how far she could trust Mr. Temple. He seemed like a good man, and plainly her father had trusted him, except in the matter of the missing ten thousand pounds (and where in the world could that be?); but she just couldn't be sure of him. He must have found out by now that she'd left Mrs. Rees's; in his anxiety about her he might go as far as to make her a ward of the court—and where would that leave her? With even less freedom than she'd had before.

No, one day she'd go to Mr. Temple and explain; but until then she'd stay with the Garlands and keep out of sight.

But how long could she stay here, with no money?

As long as she wished, if she worked for it.

She washed the dishes and sat down to draft a series of

advertisements for all the major papers. That cheered her up again; and then a customer came to book a portrait sitting for himself and his fiancée, and Sally took a leaf out of Trembler's book and sold him a stereoscope. They would soon have the finest selection of stereographs in London, she told him. He went away impressed.

But eventually she found herself turning back to the Nightmare: to the stifling heat, the darkness, the familiar hideous fear . . . And the new elements: the voices . . .

"Where is it?"

"Not with me! I pray—I beg of you—it is with a friend—"

"They are coming! Be quick!"

Voices she could understand, though they weren't speaking in English—a strange sensation, like seeing through a wall. But of course! It was Hindustani! She and her father had used it as a secret language when she was younger. And *it*—what could *it* be, that was with a friend? Could it be the ruby? Impossible to tell. And her father's face, so young, so fierce; and the voice which now, after that bleak day at Swaleness, she knew was that of Major Marchbanks . . .

A chill gradually crept over her that no amount of coal on the kitchen fire could dispel. Something had happened in those few minutes, sixteen years ago, which had led after all this time to pursuit and danger and death. Maybe to more deaths than one. And if she wanted to know more, she'd have to enter the Nightmare again . . .

She shivered and sat down to wait for the others to come back.

THAT DAY, Jim Taylor took an unauthorized afternoon off. It was a simple enough dodge: he just walked out of the building with a fake parcel, as if he was going to the post office, and left two or three contradictory messages behind about where he was and who'd sent him. He'd used the trick before, but he didn't want to do it too often.

A train from London Bridge Station took him out along the same dreary stretch of coastline that Sally had traveled, toward Swaleness. He wanted to have a look around; and besides, he had an idea. It was a penny dreadful idea, but a good one. It involved a lot of waiting about, and the exercise of a great deal of persuasion, but in the end he knew he'd been right. As he sat in the train going back (rather more carefully than Sally) he wondered what it might lead to, but he wasn't in any real doubt. After all, here was something straight out of *Stirring Tales for British Lads*, or *The Adventures of Jack Harkaway*—the penny dreadful once again proving to be a sound and accurate guide to life. And the penny dreadful line on anything Eastern was unequivocal: it meant trouble.

Trouble, in particular, for Sally, to whom Jim had conceived a fierce attachment in the past week or so.

I'll keep it to meself for the time being, he thought. *It'll be safer all 'round. There'll be plenty of time to tell her later on.*

MEANWHILE, Mrs. Holland had had some news.

One of the agents she sometimes employed, a villain called Jonathan Berry, came to see her at about the same time as the Reverend Bedwell called at Burton Street.

Mr. Berry was a huge man, six and a half feet tall and broad in proportion; he filled the narrow hall of Holland's Lodgings and terrified Adelaide. He picked her up with one hand and held her close to his dirty ear.

"M-M-Mrs. Holland's with the gentleman, sir," she whispered, beginning to sob.

"Go and get her," growled Mr. Berry. "There ain't no gentleman here, you lying little earwig."

He dropped her. She scrambled away like a mouse, and he laughed—a sinister rumbling sound, like a subterranean fall of rock.

Mrs. Holland was not pleased to be called away. Bedwell was talking, in his confusion, of a figure called Ah Ling, whose name never appeared without a tremor of fear; a junk came into the story, and a knife, and lights below the water, and all manner of things. She cursed, and told Adelaide to stay and listen careful. Adelaide waited until the old woman had left and then lay down beside the sweating, murmuring figure of the sailor and cried in earnest, clinging to his unheeding hand.

"Mr. Berry, I declare," said Mrs. Holland to the visitor, having inserted her teeth. "You been out long?"

She was referring to the Dartmoor jail.

"I been out since August, ma'am." Mr. Berry was on his best behavior; he had even taken off his greasy cap and was twisting it nervously as he sat in the small armchair that Mrs. Holland offered him in the parlor. "I hear as you're interested in who killed Henry Hopkins," he went on.

"I may be, Mr. Berry."

"Well, I heard as how Solomon Lieber—"

"The pawnbroker, of Wormwood Street?"

"That's him. Well, I heard as he pawned a diamond pin yesterday, the very double of the one Hopkins used to wear."

Mrs. Holland was up at once.

"You busy, Mr. Berry? Care for a stroll?"

"Nothing I'd like better, Mrs. Holland."

"Adelaide!" called the lady from the hall. "I'm going out. Don't you let no one in."

"A DIAMOND PIN, lady?" said the ancient pawnbroker. "Got a lovely one here. Present for your gentleman friend?" he asked, squinting up at Mr. Berry.

Mr. Berry's reply was to seize the cotton muffler hanging loosely around the old man's neck and drag him right over the counter, knocking off a shelf full of watches and a tray of rings.

"We don't want to buy one, we want to see the one you pawned yesterday," he said.

"Certainly, sir! Wouldn't dream of objecting!" gasped the old man, clutching weakly at Mr. Berry's jacket to avoid being strangled. His legs were caught on the counter; Mr. Berry dropped him, and he crashed to the floor.

"Oh, please—please don't hurt me—please, sir—don't knock me about—I beg you, sir! My old wife—"

He was shaking and stammering and trying to pull himself up by Mr. Berry's trousers. Berry kicked him away.

"Bring your wife in here, and I'll pull her legs off," he growled. "Find that pin, quick."

The pawnbroker opened a drawer with trembling hands and held out a pin.

"That the one, ma'am?" said Mr. Berry, taking it.

Mrs. Holland peered closely. "That's it. Now, who brought it in, Mr. Lieber? If you can't remember, Mr. Berry might be able to help."

Mr. Berry took a step toward him, and the old man nodded vigorously.

"Course I remember," he said. "Name of Ernie Blackett. Young chap. Croke's Court, Seven Dials."

"Thank you, Mr. Lieber," said Mrs. Holland. "I can see you're a sensible man. You got to be careful who you lends your money to. You won't mind if I takes the pin, will you?"

"It ain't—I mean I've only had it a day—I ain't allowed to sell it yet—it's the law, ma'am," he said desperately.

"Well, I'm not buying it," she said, "so that's all right, ain't it? Good morning, Mr. Lieber."

She left, and Mr. Berry, after absently emptying several other drawers on the floor, breaking half a dozen umbrellas, and knocking Mr. Lieber's legs from under him, followed her out of the little shop.

"Seven Dials," she said. "Let's get the omnibus, Mr. Berry. Me legs ain't what they was."

"Nor's his," said Mr. Berry, rumbling with admiration for the quickness of his own wit.

CROKE'S COURT, Seven Dials, was as crowded and villainous a warren as you could find in the whole of London; but its villainy was different from Wapping's. The closeness of the river lent a certain nautical dash to the crimes that flourished around Hangman's Wharf, whereas Seven Dials was merely sordid and metropolitan. Besides, Mrs. Holland was out of her territory there.

However, the massive presence of Mr. Berry made up for that. By the exercise of his charm, they very soon found the room they were looking for—in a tenement inhabited by an Irishman, his wife, their eight children, a blind musician, two flower girls, a seller of printed ballads and murderers' last confessions, and a Punch and Judy man. The room in question was pointed out to them by the Irishman's wife.

Mr. Berry kicked open the door, and they entered to find a fat youth asleep on a filthy bed. He stirred, but did not wake.

Mr. Berry sniffed the air. "Drunk," he announced. "Disgustin'."

"Wake him up, Mr. Berry," said Mrs. Holland.

Mr. Berry lifted the foot of the bed and tipped it— sleeper, blankets, and all—in a struggling heap on the floor.

"Wossat?" said the youth, his mouth full of pillow.

For an answer, Mr. Berry picked him up and flung him at the only other piece of furniture the room possessed, a rickety chest of drawers. This promptly split asunder; the youth sprawled groaning among the fragments.

"Get up," said Mr. Berry. "Where's yer manners?"

The youth struggled up, supporting himself on the wall. The fright, on top of what must have been a substantial hangover, had turned his face a distinctive shade of green. He looked blearily at his visitors.

"Who are yer?" he managed to say.

Mrs. Holland tutted. "Now then," she said. "What d'you know about Henry Hopkins?"

"Nuffink," said the youth, and Mr. Berry hit him. "Gerroff! Ow—leave me alone!"

Mrs. Holland took out the diamond pin.

"What about this, then?"

His narrow eyes flicked to it painfully.

"I never seen it in me life," he said, and flinched. But

this time Mr. Berry merely wagged a finger at him.

"You want to think hard," he said. "You're a disappointment to us, you are."

And then he hit him. The youth fell to his knees, sniveling.

"All right, I found it. I took it to Solly Lieber's and he give me a fiver for it. That's all, honest!" he wailed.

"Where'd you get it?"

"I told you, I found it!"

Mrs. Holland sighed. Shaking his head at the stubborn wickedness of human nature, Mr. Berry hit him again; and this time the youth lost his temper. He shot across the room like a rat and delved swiftly into the wreckage of the chest of drawers, coming up with a pistol.

His two visitors fell still.

"You come any closer and I'll b-b-bloody shoot," he said.

"Go on, then," said Mr. Berry.

"I will! I will!"

Mr. Berry reached forward and plucked the gun out of his hand like an apple from a tree. The youth collapsed.

"Shall I hit him again, ma'am?" inquired Mr. Berry.

"No! No! Don't hit me!" quavered the youth. "I'll tell yer everything!"

"Hit him anyway," said Mrs. Holland, taking the pistol. That formality completed, she went on: "What else did you take from Henry Hopkins?"

"The pin. The shooter," he sobbed. "A couple o' sovereigns. A watch and chain and a silver flask."

"What else?"

"Nothing, ma'am, I swear it."

"No pieces of paper?"

The youth gaped.

"Aha," said Mrs. Holland. "Go on, Mr. Berry, do as yer like, only leave him with a voice."

"No! No! Please!" cried Ernie Blackett as Mr. Berry raised his fist. "Here y'are—take 'em! Take 'em!"

He scrabbled at a pocket and threw down three or four scraps of paper and then turned away, shaking. Mrs. Holland snatched them up and scanned them while Mr. Berry waited.

She looked up. "Is that all? Nothing else?"

"Not a bleedin' thing, I swear it! Honest!"

"Ah, but you ain't honest," said Mrs. Holland severely. "That's the trouble. Well, come on, Mr. Berry. We'll take the pistol, to remind us of our good friend Henry Hopkins. Deceased."

She hobbled to the door and waited on the malodorous landing while Mr. Berry spoke to their host.

"I don't like to see a young man of your age drinking," he said solemnly. "It's the young man's ruin, drink is. I could tell you was drunk as soon as I come in. The smallest glass of drink is the first step on the road to madness, hallucinations, softening of the brain, and moral decay. It'd break your heart to know how many men's lives have been ruined through drink. Keep off it, is my advice. Go and sign the pledge, like I done. You'll be a better man for it. Here—" He fumbled at an inside pocket. "I'll leave you a useful tract, what'll help you improve. It's called 'The Drunkard's Lament, by One Who Has Seen the Blessed Light.'"

He tucked the precious document into Ernie Blackett's nerveless hand and joined Mrs. Holland on the stairs.

"That it, Mrs. Holland?"

"That's it, Mr. Berry. She's cleverer than I took her for, the little bitch."

"Eh?"

"Nevermind . . . Back to Wapping, Mr. Berry."

It was well for Ernie Blackett that he had owned up and given Mrs. Holland the pieces of paper. Her next step would have been to tell Mr. Berry to search him; and when they were found, Ernie would swiftly have joined Henry Hopkins in that corner of the afterlife reserved for metropolitan minor criminals, where they could have improved their brief acquaintance. As it was, he came quite well out of the transaction, with only two broken ribs, a black eye, and a temperance tract for punishment.

12

--- ◆ ---

Substitution

JUST AS MRS. HOLLAND AND MR. BERRY BOARDED THE
omnibus back to Wapping, a cab drew up at Hangman's
Wharf. Frederick Garland asked the driver to wait, and
Mr. Bedwell knocked on the door of Holland's Lodgings.

Frederick looked to the left and right. The little row of
buildings stood just behind Wapping High Street and
seemed to be crowded so close to the river that a slight
push would send them in. Holland's Lodgings was the
dirtiest and narrowest and most decrepit of them all.

"No reply?" he said as Mr. Bedwell knocked again.

"Lying low, I expect," said the curate, trying the door
and finding it bolted. "This is awkward. What do we do
now?"

"Climb in," said Frederick. "We know he's in there,
after all."

He was looking up at the side of the building. Between
Holland's Lodgings and the house next door a narrow
passage a little over two feet in width ran down to the
open river, where the masts of boats were clustered. At
second-floor level a small window overlooked the passage.

"Can you manage?" said the curate.

"Just keep knocking. Make a row, so no one'll notice what I'm up to."

Frederick had climbed mountains both in Scotland and in Switzerland, and it was the work of a minute to push himself, back against one wall and feet against the other, up the gap between the houses. Opening the window took a little longer, maneuvering himself through longer still, but eventually he stood on the narrow landing, listening hard.

The curate was still pounding on the front door, but apart from that the house was silent. Frederick ran downstairs and unbolted the door.

"Well done!" said Mr. Bedwell, stepping in quickly.

"It looks as if the old woman's out," said Frederick. "But according to Sally's friend Jim, the little girl Adelaide hardly ever leaves the place. . . ."

They looked quickly in the downstairs rooms and then searched the second floor, but found nothing. They were about to go up to the next when there was a knock on the front door.

They looked at each other.

"Wait here," said the curate.

He ran down swiftly. Frederick listened, pressed against the angle of the landing.

" 'Ow long you going to keep me?" demanded the cab driver. " 'Cause I'll have something on account, if you don't mind. This ain't the best part o' London to hang about in."

"Here," said Bedwell. "Take this, and wait by the pavement on the other side of the swingbridge we came over. If we're not out in half an hour, you may go."

He shut the door again and ran back up. Frederick held up a hand.

"Listen," he whispered, pointing. "In there."

They moved up, treading as lightly as possible on the bare boards. A man's voice was murmuring indistinctly behind one of the doors, and they could hear a child saying "Shh ... shh ..." They stood outside the room for a moment. Bedwell was listening intently.

Then he looked at Frederick and nodded. Frederick opened the door.

The stale smoky reek made them both wrinkle their nostrils. A child—or not so much a child as a pair of wide eyes surrounded by dirt—gazed at them in terror. And on the bed lay the double of the curate.

Bedwell threw himself down and shook his brother by the shoulders. The child backed away silently, and Frederick marveled at the extraordinary resemblance between the two men. It was not even a resemblance—it was an identity.

Nicholas was trying to lift his brother up, and the other was shaking his head and pushing him away.

"Matthew! Matthew!" said the curate. "It's me, it's Nicky! Come on, old man! Snap out of it—open your eyes and look! See who it is!"

But Matthew was in another world. Nicholas let him fall and looked up bitterly.

"Hopeless," he said. "We'll have to carry him."

"Are you Adelaide?" Frederick said to the child.

She nodded.

"Where's Mrs. Holland?"

"I dunno," she whispered.

"Is she in?"

Adelaide shook her head.

"Well, that's something at least. Now listen, Adelaide, we're going to take Mr. Bedwell away—"

She clung to Matthew at once, her little arms tight around his neck.

"No!" she cried. "She'll kill me!"

And at the sound of her voice, Matthew Bedwell woke up. He sat up and put an arm around her—and then saw his brother and fell still, speechless.

"It's all right, old fellow," said Nicholas. "I've come to take you home. . . ."

The sailor's eyes moved to Frederick, and Adelaide clung more tightly than ever, whispering, "Please don't go—she'll kill me if you ain't here—she will—"

"Adelaide, we've got to take Mr. Bedwell away," said Frederick gently. "He's not well. He can't stay here. Mrs. Holland's keeping him here against the law—"

"She said I wasn't to let no one in! She'll kill me!"

The child was nearly distracted with fear, and Matthew Bedwell stroked her hair mechanically, struggling to understand what was happening.

And then the curate held up his hand for silence.

They could hear footsteps and voices from the ground floor; and then a cracked old voice shouted, "Adelaide!"

The child whimpered and shrank toward the wall. Frederick took her arm and said softly, "Is there a back staircase?"

She nodded. Frederick turned to Nicholas Bedwell and saw that the curate was already on his feet.

"Yes," he said, "I'll go and pretend to be him. I'll keep her busy while you get him out the back way. It's all right, my dear," he said to Adelaide. "She'll never know the difference."

"But she's got—" Adelaide began, intending to say something about Mr. Berry; but then the old woman shouted again, and she shrank into silence.

The curate left the room swiftly. They heard him run along the landing and then start down the stairs, and Frederick tugged at Matthew Bedwell. The sailor rose shakily to his feet.

"Come on," said Frederick. "We'll get you out. But you've got to move briskly and keep quiet."

The sailor nodded. "Come on, Adelaide," he mumbled. "Show us the way, girl."

Adelaide whispered, "I daren't."

"You've got to," said Bedwell. "Else I'll be cross. Get a move on."

She scrambled up and ran through the door. Bedwell followed, gathering up a canvas kit bag, and Frederick went after them, pausing to listen. He heard the curate's voice and Mrs. Holland's cracked reply; why were they all so afraid of her?

Adelaide led the way down a staircase even narrower and dirtier than the other one. They stopped in the passage on the ground floor. The curate's voice, slurred and roughened, came from somewhere near the front door, and Frederick whispered to the child, "Show us the back way out."

Trembling, she opened the kitchen door, and they went through.

And found themselves face-to-face with Mr. Berry.

He was setting a kettle on the fire. He looked up and gazed at them, and a little frown gathered itself effortfully on his rocky forehead.

Frederick thought quickly.

"How do," he said, nodding. "Which way's the back yard, mate?"

"Out there," said the big man, inclining his head.

Frederick nudged Bedwell, who moved forward with

him, and took Adelaide's hand. She came unwillingly. Mr. Berry watched dumbly as they walked out of the kitchen, and then sat down to light a pipe.

They found themselves in a dark little yard. Adelaide was clinging to Frederick's hand and, he saw, trembling violently. She had gone white.

"What is it?" he said.

She could not even speak. She was terrified. Frederick looked around; there was a brick wall about six feet in height on one side, and what looked like an alley beyond.

"Bedwell," he said, "jump up and take the girl. Adelaide, you're coming with us. You can't stay here to be frightened like this."

Bedwell scrambled up, and then Frederick saw that Adelaide's fear was focused on a patch of bare earth by the wall. He hoisted her up to Bedwell and then scrambled over himself.

Bedwell was swaying and looking ill. Frederick looked back; he was anxious about the curate and what would happen when Mrs. Holland discovered the truth. But for the moment he had a sick man and a terrified child to look after, and the likelihood of pursuit at any moment.

"Come on," he said. "There's a cab waiting on the other side of the bridge. Let's be off."

He hurried them out of the alley and away.

SALLY, busy with the wording of an advertisement, looked up in surprise as Frederick staggered into the shop half-carrying the unconscious Bedwell. At first she didn't see the child who followed them.

"Mr. Bedwell!" she said. "What's happened? Or is it—"

"This is the brother, Sally. Look—I've got to go back

straight away. The other half of the family's still there, bluffing it out—but there's a huge ugly bruiser in the house—and I had to take the cab to get these two here— oh, this is Adelaide. She's coming to live with us."

He laid the sailor on the floor and ran out. The cab whirled him away at once.

MUCH LATER, he returned. He had the Reverend Nicholas with him, and the parson had a black eye.

"What a fight!" he said. "Sally, you should have seen it! Horatius at the bridge had nothing on it. I got back just in time—"

"He did indeed," said the curate. "But how's Matthew?"

"In bed, asleep. But—"

"Is Adelaide all right?" said Frederick. "I couldn't leave her there. She was terrified."

"She's with Trembler. Your eye, Mr. Bedwell! It's terribly bruised—come and sit down. Let me look at it. What on earth happened?"

They went through into the kitchen, where Adelaide and Trembler were having some tea. Trembler poured out a cup for each of the men as the curate explained what had taken place.

"I kept her talking while the others left. Then I let her put me back to bed. I pretended to be incoherent. She went out to look for Adelaide and I got up and tried to leave, and that's when she set the big fellow on to me."

"He's a monster," said Frederick. "But you were holding him off. I heard the row from the street outside and just kicked my way in. What a fight!"

"He was strong, but that's all. No speed, no science.

Outside in the street, or in the ring, I'd have given him a run for his money, but there wasn't enough space in there; if he'd cornered me, I wouldn't have got out alive."

"What about Mrs. Holland?" asked Sally.

The two men looked at each other.

"Well, she had a gun," said Frederick.

"Garland hit the big fellow over the head with a length of wood from the broken banisters, and he went down like an ox. And then Mrs. Holland produced her pistol. She'd have shot me, too, if you hadn't knocked it out of her hand," added the clergyman to Frederick.

"A little pearl-handled one," said Frederick. "Does she always carry a pistol?" he asked Adelaide.

"I dunno," the child whispered.

"Anyway, she said . . ." He paused, looking unhappy, and then went on to Sally, "She said she'd find you out, wherever you are, and kill you. She told me to tell you. Whether she knows where you are or is just guessing, I've no idea. But she doesn't know who I am or where we live—she can't. You're quite safe here, and so's Adelaide. She'll never find you."

"She will," whispered Adelaide.

"How's she going to do that?" said Trembler. "You're as safe here as the Bank of England. Let me tell you something—I'm on the run meself, just like Miss Sally and you, and I ain't been found yet. So you stay here with us, and you'll be all right."

"Are you Miss Lockhart?" said Adelaide to Sally.

"That's right," said Sally.

"She will find me," Adelaide whispered. "If I went to the bottom of the sea she'd find me and drag me out. She would."

"Well, we won't let her," said Sally.

"But she's after you, too, ain't she? She said she's going to kill yer. She sent Henry Hopkins to do an accident, only he got killed."

"Henry Hopkins?"

"She told him to steal a bit o' paper off you. And he had to make an accident happen and finish you off."

"That's where she got the pistol from," said Sally weakly. "*My* pistol . . ."

" 'S all right," said Trembler, unconvincingly. "She won't find you here, miss."

"She will," said Adelaide again. "She knows everythink. Everythink and everyone. She's got a knife in her bag what she cut the last little girl open with. She showed me. There ain't nothing she don't know, or anyone. All the streets in London and all the ships in the docks. And now I've run away she'll sharpen her knife. She said she would. She's got a stone for sharpenin' it, and a box to put me in, and a place in the yard to bury me. She showed me where I was going to lie when she'd done with cutting me up. Her last little girl's lying in the yard. I hates to go out there."

The others were silent. Adelaide's mothlike little voice came to a stop, and she sat hunched over, her eyes on the floor. Trembler reached across the table.

"Here," he said. "Eat yer bun, there's a good girl."

She picked at it for a minute.

Mr. Bedwell said, "I'll go up and see to my brother, if I may."

Sally jumped up. "I'll show you where he is," she said, and took him upstairs.

"Fast asleep," he said when he came out. "I've seen him

like this before. He'll probably sleep for twenty-four hours."

"Well, we'll post him on to you when he wakes up," said Frederick. "At least you know where he is. You'll stay the night? Good. My word, I'm hungry. Trembler, what about some kippers? Adelaide, you're going to live with us from now on. You can make yourself useful by finding some cups and plates and things. Sally—she'll need something to wear. There's a secondhand clothes shop around the corner—Trembler'll show you where it is."

THE WEEKEND passed quietly. Rosa, after her first astonishment at finding the house full, took to Adelaide at once, and seemed to know all kinds of things that Sally did not, such as how to make Adelaide wash herself, and what time she should go to bed, and how to trim her hair and choose clothes for her. Sally wanted to help; but she couldn't discover how to express the kindness she felt, whereas Rosa would hug and kiss the child on impulse, or fluff out her hair, or chat about the theater. And Trembler told her jokes or taught her card games.

So while Adelaide became more confident with those two, she was ill at ease with Sally and fell silent when they were alone together. Sally would have been hurt by this if Rosa had let her, but the older girl took care to include her in every conversation and to consult her about Adelaide's future.

"Do you know, she's got no idea of anything?" Rosa said to her on Sunday evening. "She doesn't know the names of any parts of London except Wapping and Shadwell—she didn't even know the name of the Queen! Sally, why don't you teach her to read and write and so forth?"

"I don't think I could . . ."

"Of course you could. You'd be perfect."

"She's frightened of me."

"She's worried about you, because of what Mrs. Holland said. And because of her gentleman. She's been up to see him a dozen times, you know. She just sits and holds his hand, and then comes away again. . . ."

Matthew Bedwell had not woken until Sunday morning, and it had been Adelaide who had woken him. But he was so disoriented that he could not take in where he was or what had happened. Sally went up to see him when he had drunk some tea, but he would not speak to her. "Dunno," he would say, or "I forget," or "My memory's gone"; and despite all Sally's efforts to prompt him with her father's name, and that of the company, and the ship, and the company's agent Mr. Van Eeden, he remained mute. Only the phrase "the Seven Blessings" provoked a response, and that was not encouraging: what little color there was in his face drained at once, and he broke into a sweat and began to tremble. Frederick advised her to leave it for a day or so.

When she'd last seen Jim, Sally had arranged to meet him again at the bandstand every Saturday afternoon. At their first rendezvous she told him about everything that had happened since she'd left Mrs. Rees's. When he heard about the rescue of Bedwell and Adelaide, he nearly wept with frustration that he'd missed it. He swore he'd be around as soon as he could, to check that these new friends of hers were all right. "You don't know who you can trust," he said.

He seemed to be on the point of saying something else,

too. Two or three times he began, and then broke off, shaking his head and saying it would keep. Finally she said, "Jim, what *is* it? Have you found something out? For heaven's sake, tell me!"

But he wouldn't. "It'll keep," he said. "No harm in waiting."

And that was all he'd say.

That weekend, the first artistic and dramatic stereographs were taken. Taking a stereograph was much easier than Sally had imagined. A stereo camera was just like an ordinary one, except that it had two lenses as far apart as a person's eyes, each taking a separate image. When the two images were printed side by side and viewed through a stereoscope, which was only a device with two lenses set at a certain angle to blend the images into one, the viewer saw a picture in three dimensions. The effect was almost magical.

Frederick set up some comic pictures first, to sell separately. One was called "A Horrid Discovery in the Kitchen," and featured Rosa as a fainting wife, with Trembler as her shocked husband. They were reacting to what Sally, as a kitchenmaid, was showing them: a cupboard from which were crawling a dozen black beetles, each the size of a goose. Adelaide had cut the beetles from brown paper and inked them black. Trembler wanted a photograph of Adelaide, too, so they dressed him up, sat her on his knee, and took a picture to illustrate a sentimental song. "Very fetching," said Frederick.

And so their weekend passed.

ELSEWHERE IN London, things were not so peaceful.

Mr. Berry, for instance, was having a rough time. Mrs.

Holland made him clear up the mess that had been made of the hall, and repair the broken banisters, and when he ventured to complain, she let him know what she thought of him.

"A big strong man like you," she said, "to let yourself be knocked about by a little whippersnapper like him? And him half-sodden with opium too! My word, I'd hate to see you tackle anything fierce, like a cockroach."

"Oh, give over, Mrs. Holland," moaned the big man nervously, nailing a batten across a broken door. "He must have bin a perfessional. It's no disgrace to be beat scientific. He's fought with the best, that one."

"Well, now he's fought with the worst. Even little Adelaide would've put up more of a scrap. Ooh, Mr. Berry, you got a lot to make up for, you have. Get on and finish that door. There's a pile o' potatoes to peel out the back."

Mr. Berry muttered to himself, but quietly. He had not dared tell her about what he had allowed to happen in the kitchen. As far as she knew, Adelaide had just vanished; but the sudden appearance of the photographer from Swaleness had reminded her of Sally again. So she had an interest in Bedwell, too, had she? And then there was what Mrs. Holland took to be Sally's cunning in substituting a piece of nonsense for the plain instructions to where the ruby was hidden. Sally had the ruby now—she must have. Well, Mrs. Holland would find her. And where she was, there would be the photographer, and Bedwell, and a fortune.

Her discontent mounted, and so did the tasks she piled on Mr. Berry. His weekend became distinctly uncomfortable.

BUT PERHAPS the most uneasy man in London that week-end was Samuel Selby. Having parted with fifty pounds, and having received in exchange Mrs. Holland's promise that she would be back soon to do further business, he was mortified too.

Accordingly, he growled at his wife and daughter, snapped at the servants, kicked the cat, and retired early on Saturday evening to the billiard room at Laburnum Lodge, his house in Dalston. There he donned a crimson velvet smoking jacket, poured himself a large glass of brandy, and potted a few balls while he tried to work out how to thwart his blackmailer.

But try as he would, he couldn't work out how she had come by her knowledge.

Nor could he guess how much she knew. The loss of the *Lavinia*, and the fraudulent insurance claim, were bad enough; but the other business, the center of it all, the business Lockhart had been on the point of discovering—she hadn't mentioned that.

Could it be that she didn't know?

Fifty pounds was a paltry sum, after all, compared to the amounts that were involved . . .

Or was she saving it up for another visit?

Or was her informant keeping it back for some purpose of his own?

Devil take it!

He plunged the cue at a white ball, missed, ripped the cloth, and broke the cue savagely over his knee before flinging himself into an armchair.

The girl—Lockhart's daughter—did she have anything to do with it?

Impossible to say.

The office boy? The porter? No, absurd. The only man in the office who knew about it was Higgs, and Higgs—

Higgs had died. While the Lockhart girl was speaking to him. Died of fright, according to the chief clerk, who'd overheard the doctor. She must have said something to startle Higgs, something her father had passed on to her; and Higgs, instead of bluffing it out, had chosen to die.

Mr. Selby snorted with contempt. But it was an interesting speculation; and maybe, after all, Mrs. Holland was not his main enemy.

Maybe he would do better to enlist her than to fight her. Repellent as she was, she had a certain style, and Mr. Selby knew a tough chicken when he saw one.

Yes! The more he thought about it, the more he liked it. He rubbed his hands together and bit off the end of a Cuban cigar, and then donned a tasseled smoking cap to keep the smell of the tobacco from his hair, before lighting the cigar and settling back to compose another letter to Mrs. Holland.

THERE WAS one person whose weekend went according to plan—according to the plans of the Peninsular and Oriental Steam Navigation Company, no less. This was a certain passenger on board the *Drummond Castle*, from Hankow—a physically striking man, big, blond, and sunburned, but with Chinese eyes. It had been rough in the Bay of Biscay, but he had not suffered. Oblivious to every discomfort, he'd made his way with a sailor's tread all over the ship, casting expert glances at the sails and the rigging; and when there was no new nautical activity to look at, he'd sat wrapped up on the boat deck, in the place he'd made his own since Singapore, reading Thomas

De Quincey's *Confessions of an English Opium-Eater*.

The cold wind and the drizzle concerned him not a bit. In fact, as the air became chillier and the sky grayer, the passenger's spirits seemed to rise. He ate and drank the more heartily as the ship plunged the more sickeningly in the Channel swell, and puffed constantly at a series of pungent black cheroots. On Sunday evening the vessel rounded the North Foreland and began the final stretch of her journey into the Thames estuary. She moved slowly in these congested waters, and as the day faded, the passenger moved to the rail and gazed with close attention at the lights of the Kent coast to the left, steady and soft and warm; at the ghostly, creaming foam thrown up by the bows of the ship; and at the myriad of winking lights from buoys and lighthouses that guided innocent travelers like himself through the shoals and hazards of the sea.

And as this thought struck him, the passenger suddenly laughed.

13

Lights Below the Water

THE OFFICE IN CHEAPSIDE HAD THE DECORATORS IN. Buckets of whitewash and distemper stood in the hall, and brushes and ladders obstructed the corridors. The place was on the point of closing on Monday evening when the porter rang for Jim.

"What d'yer want?" Jim demanded, and noticed a messenger boy standing by the porter's fire. Jim eyed him disfavorably, paying particular attention to his pillbox hat.

"Letter for Mr. Selby," said the porter. "Take it up, and look smart."

"What's he waiting for?" said Jim, indicating the messenger boy. "Waiting for his master, with the barrel organ, is he?"

"None o' your business," said the messenger boy.

"That's right," said the porter. "This is a smart lad, this one. He'll go a long way."

"Well, why don't he start now?"

" 'Cause he's waiting for an answer, that's why."

The messenger boy smirked, and Jim left, scowling.

"He wants an answer, Mr. Selby," he said in the front office. "He's waiting down there now."

"Is he," said Mr. Selby, ripping open the envelope. His cheeks were highly colored today, and his eyes were bloodshot; Jim observed this with interest, wondering whether Mr. Selby was likely to expire from apoplexy. Then, as he watched, the phenomenon altered, and Mr. Selby's countenance suffered a sea change: the high tide of his color went out all at once, leaving a gray-white expanse fringed with ginger whiskers. Their owner sat down suddenly.

"Here," he said in a hoarse voice. "Who's downstairs? The man himself?"

"A messenger boy, Mr. Selby."

"Oh. Here—nip over to that window smartish and have a look outside."

Jim did so. The street was dark, and the lights in the office windows and on the front of the carriages and omnibuses shone warmly in the gloom.

"Can you see a feller—cleanshaven—fair hair—sunburned complexion—stoutish? A Chinese kind of look about him?"

"There's hundreds of people about, Mr. Selby. What might he be wearing?"

"I don't know what he'd be bloody wearing, boy! Is there anyone standing about, waiting?"

"No one like that."

"Hmm. Well, I better write an answer, I suppose."

He hastily scribbled something and thrust it into an envelope.

"Give this to him," he said.

"Ain't you going to write the address, Mr. Selby?"

"What for? The boy knows where to take it."

"In case he drops down dead in the street. He's a

sickly-looking blighter. I shouldn't be surprised if he was to sling his hook before the week's out—"

"Oh, get out of it!"

Thus prevented from discovering the name of the man who was making Mr. Selby so anxious, Jim tried another tack with the messenger boy.

"Here," he said ingratiatingly. "I wonder as if you'd have any use for this? You're welcome to it if you'd like it."

He held out a tattered copy of *The Skeleton Crew, or Wildfire Ned*. The messenger boy cast a cold eye on it and took it without a word, tucking it into his inside pocket.

"Where's the answer what I was waiting for?" he said.

"Oh, yes, how silly of me," said Jim. "Here it is. Only Mr. Selby's forgot to write the gentleman's name on the envelope. I'll do it for yer, if yer just tell me what it is," he offered, dipping a pen in the porter's inkwell.

"Get stuffed," said the messenger boy. "Give it here. I knows where to take it."

"Well, o' course you do," said Jim, handing it over. "I only thought as it'd be more businesslike."

"Bollocks to that," said the messenger boy, and left the fireside. Jim was opening the door for him; there seemed to be some obstruction in the way, and he bent to clear it. The porter was complimenting the messenger boy on his smart uniform.

"Yes, well, there's an art in wearing clothes, I always say," said the visitor. "You keep yourself smart, and you'll get on."

"Yus, there's a lot in that," said the porter. "You listenin', Jim? Here's a young lad with an 'ead on his shoulders."

"Yes, Mr. Buxton," said Jim respectfully. "I shall remember that. Here—I'll show you out."

With a friendly hand on the boy's back, Jim opened the door and showed him into the street. The messenger boy stalked off without a word, but before he had gone five yards, Jim called out:

"Here! Ain't you forgotten something?"

"What?" said the boy, turning.

"This," said Jim, and released a pellet heavily charged with ink from his India rubber band. It hit the messenger boy right between the eyes, splashing its load all over his nose and cheeks and forehead and making him howl with rage. Jim stood on the step shaking his head.

The messenger boy ground his teeth and clenched his fists, but the sight of Jim's bright eyes and tense form, balanced and waiting for him, made him consider that dignity was the better part of vengeance; and he turned and walked away without a word. Jim watched with great satisfaction as the smart maroon jacket, with its newly imprinted handprint in sticky whitewash, disappeared into the crowd.

"THE WARWICK HOTEL," said Jim to Sally two hours later. "He had it on his hat, silly bugger. And on all his buttons. I wouldn't half like to see what happens when he goes in the hotel with ink and whitewash all over him. Here, Adelaide," he went on. "I been down Wapping."

"Did yer see Mrs. Holland?" said the child.

"Just once. She's got that big bloke with her, and he's doing all your chores. Here! This is a good un!"

They were in the kitchen at Burton Street, and he was looking at the freshly printed stereographs.

"Which one's that?" said Sally, interested to see which one found most favor.

"These bloody great beetles. That's a laugh, that is. You oughter do murders. You oughter do Sweeney Todd—or the Red Barn."

"We will," said Sally.

"Or Spring-Heeled Jack flying through the air."

"Who?" said Frederick.

"Here," said Jim, offering a copy of *Boys of England*. Frederick put his feet on the coal scuttle and settled back comfortably to read it.

"But what about your bloke upstairs?" Jim went on. "How's he doing?"

"He's hardly spoken," said Sally.

"What's the matter with him? Is he frightened o' something? You'd think he was safe enough here."

"Perhaps he just needs to recover from the opium. Or perhaps we ought to give him some more," said Sally, who was very conscious of the little brown ball of resin in the kitchen cupboard. For her Nightmare was imprisoned in it like a genie in a lamp, and needed only the application of a match for its release. "What do you think the man in the Warwick Hotel wants?" she said, to change the subject.

"Old Selby's dead jumpy these days. I thought he was going to keel over when he read the letter this afternoon. He's double-crossing 'em, and they've twigged it; that's all it is."

"What can they be doing, though? Frederick, what can a firm of shipping agents do that breaks the law? What crimes can they commit?"

"Smuggling," he said. "How's that?"

"Could be," said Jim. "Then there's fraud. Sinking ships, and claiming on the insurance."

"No," said Sally. "The firm only had the one ship. They're not shipowners, they're shipping agents. And that sort of thing's too easy to spot, surely?"

"It happens all the time," said Jim.

"You think it was sunk on purpose?" said Frederick.

"Course it was."

"What for?"

"I can tell you," said the voice of Matthew Bedwell.

HE STOOD in the kitchen doorway, pale and trembling. Adelaide gasped, and Frederick jumped up at once and helped him to a chair by the fire.

"Where am I?" he said. "How long have I been under?"

"You're in Bloomsbury," said Frederick. "Your brother brought you here three days ago. We're all friends— you're quite safe."

Bedwell looked at Adelaide, who said nothing.

"Adelaide ran away," said Sally. "Mr. Garland is letting us stay here because we've got nowhere else to go. Apart from Jim, that is."

The sailor's eyes moved painfully from one to another of them.

"You were saying something about the *Lavinia*," he said. "That's right, isn't it?"

"Yes," said Sally. "What can you tell us about it?"

He focused on her. "Are you Mr. Lockhart's girl?"

She nodded.

"He asked—he asked me to bring you a message. I'm afraid he's . . . I'm afraid they . . . What I mean to say is, he's dead, miss. I'm sorry. I guess you knew."

She nodded again, and found herself unable to speak.

Bedwell looked at Frederick. "Is my brother here?"

"He's in Oxford. He's waiting for you to get better. He'll be coming here on Wednesday, but perhaps you'll be able to go there before then."

Bedwell leaned back and closed his eyes. "Maybe," he said.

"Are you hungry?" said Sally. "You haven't eaten for days."

"If you've such a thing as a tot of brandy in the house, I'll be mighty obliged to you. But I couldn't eat at the moment. Not even your soup, Adelaide."

"It ain't *mine*," said the child vehemently.

Frederick poured a small glass of brandy.

"Your good health," said Bedwell, and swallowed half. "Yes," he said, "the *Lavinia*. . . . I'll tell you what I know about her."

"What about the message?" said Sally.

"That's part of it. I'll start at Singapore, where your father joined the ship."

"I WAS THE second mate of the *Lavinia*," he began. "Not much of a berth, since she was only a shabby little tramp—all kinds of goods between Yokohama and Calcutta, and pretty well anywhere else on the way. But I'd had a bit of bad luck; and there was the *Lavinia* in need of a second mate, and myself in need of a job. . . . I was with her for two months before she sank.

"Now, she had a bit of a reputation, the *Lavinia*. Not so much her as the owners, perhaps. There's rogues enough in the China Sea, God knows, from smugglers to pirates to every kind of cutthroat—but Lockhart and Selby were a stranger kind of crook than that. Worse, maybe."

"Not my father," said Sally fiercely.

"No," said Bedwell, "I grant you that. Your father was a good man—I learned that within two days of his coming aboard. It was other men using his name and the firm's that brought it the reputation it had."

"But what was this reputation?" said Frederick.

Bedwell looked at his glass, and Sally filled it.

"I don't know what you know about the Chinese in the East Indies," he said. "There's all kinds of networks of influence and pressure—political, commercial, criminal.... And there are the secret societies. They started, so they say, as a way of organizing resistance to the Manchu dynasty that rules China. And I daresay some of 'em are innocent enough—just a way of looking after your own people or your relatives, with a bit of ritual thrown in. But there's others far more sinister than that. The Triads, they're called—"

"I know 'em!" said Jim suddenly. "The Black Dragon Society! And the Brothers of the Scarlet Hand! There was a story about them in *Stirring Tales for British Lads*."

"Oh, hush, Jim," said Sally. "This is serious. Go on, Mr. Bedwell."

"I don't suppose your penny magazine knows the half of it, my lad. Murder—torture—I'd sooner fall into the hands of the Spanish Inquisition than cross the Triad Societies."

"But what's the connection with Lockhart and Selby?" Sally asked.

"Well, the word was that the firm—its agents and its

directors—was bound up with one of these societies. Under the orders of its leaders."

"What!" said Frederick.

"All of them?" said Sally. "Even a man called Hendrik Van Eeden? My father said he could be trusted."

"I don't know him, Miss Lockhart. But there are dozens of agents, and this was only a rumor. Very likely your father was right."

"What happened when he joined the ship?"

"Well, the first thing that happened was that we lost a cargo. Mr. Lockhart came aboard unexpectedly. He had a servant with him—a Malayan fellow called Perak. Never used to leave his side. Anyway, we were due to take on a cargo of cloth, and it was suddenly canceled. We were given orders to sail out in ballast, and then that was canceled, too. Finally we shifted to another berth and took a load of manganese on board. We were in harbor for a week."

"Who gave these orders?" said Frederick. "Mr. Lockhart?"

"No. The local agent. Mr. Lockhart was angry, and went back and forth I don't know how many times between the harbor and the office. I didn't blame him; I didn't like that way of running things—it was unbusinesslike and careless. Nor did he, and I guess he saw my feelings. It was during that week that we got talking. Perak the servant used to make notes—he'd been a clerk, Mr. Lockhart said.

"Anyway, we finally set sail from Singapore on June the twenty-eighth, intending to sail to Shanghai with this load of manganese. And on the first afternoon out, we saw the black junk.

"Now, those seas are mighty busy, of course, and a junk is only what you expect in that part of the world; but I didn't like the look of this one. High in the water, with a dark hull and sails, and an air of watching us. She stayed abeam for two days and nights, and we could have out-sailed her easily—that high hull means they catch all the wind, and they can't tack like a schooner. We should have left her behind and made good speed to the northeast, but we didn't.

"The fact was, the captain seemed to be dawdling on purpose. Mr. Lockhart was no sailor, else he'd have seen at once that we weren't making anything like the speed we could—and the captain, a man called Cartwright, did what he could to keep me out of Mr. Lockhart's way. Anyway, he spent most of the time in his cabin, writing up his notes.

"That was a strange time. Drifting, almost, farther and farther away from the shipping lanes, while little by little all the work on board came to an end. . . . I kept on at the captain, but he brushed me aside. The men just lay about in the shade, while that ugly black hull was never off the horizon. Just crawling, creeping, dawdling across the water . . . It was beginning to drive me mad.

"Then on the second night it happened.

"I was standing the middle watch. It was about one in the morning; a sailor called Harding was at the wheel, and that cursed black junk was still hulking in the darkness off to port. Except that it wasn't dark. There was no moon, but the stars—you've never seen stars, if you've only seen 'em from England. They don't twinkle faintly in the trop-ics, they blaze; and the sea . . . it was alive with phos-phorescence. Our wake and our bow-wave were great swirling tracks made up of billions of spots of white light, and all the sea on both sides was full of deep glowing movements—fishes darting through the depths, great shimmering clouds and veils of shadowy color, little surges and whirlpools of light far below—once or twice in your life you get a night like that, and it's a sight to leave you breathless. And the junk was the only thing in the whole glowing panorama that was dark. They had one reedy little yellow lantern swinging at the masthead—the rest was solid blackness, like a paper cutout; like a puppet in one of the shadow plays they have out there.

"And then Harding, the helmsman, says to me: 'Mr. Bedwell, there's a man moving about amidships.'

"I went to the rail, careful not to make a sound, and sure enough I saw a figure by the portside rail—in the act of climbing over, and down into a boat bobbing by the side. I was about to call out—but in all that great wash of light, I recognized his face. It was the captain.

"I told Harding to stay where he was and raced down the companionway to Mr. Lockhart's cabin. It was locked—there was no answer when I banged on it, so I kicked the door down. And then—"

He stopped and looked at Sally.

"I'm sorry, miss. He'd been stabbed."

Sally felt a rush of anguish sweep up her chest, and tears flooded her eyes and blurred the little room. She shook her head angrily.

"Go on," she said. "Don't stop."

"The cabin was overturned. All his papers were scattered on the floor, the bunk was torn open, his trunk was upside down—it was in chaos. And with the captain leaving the ship, and the junk nearby . . . I was about to turn and run out to waken the crew, when I heard a groan from the bunk.

"He was alive. Only just, but he stirred, and I tried to lift him up, but he shook his head.

" 'Who did this, Mr. Lockhart?' I said.

"He said something I couldn't catch, and then he came out with two words that made my blood run cold. 'Ah Ling,' he said. 'The black junk—it's his. The captain . . .'

"He could say no more for the moment. My mind was racing; Ah Ling—if it *was* his ship, then we were done for. Ah Ling was the most murderous, bloodthirsty savage in the South China Sea. I'd heard his name scores of times, and it was never spoken without a shudder.

"And then Mr. Lockhart spoke again. 'Find my daughter, Bedwell. My daughter Sally. Tell her what happened.' I'm sorry, Miss Lockhart; he said some more things then, and they were all jumbled—or else I couldn't hear him clearly . . . I don't know. But he finished up, 'Tell her to keep her powder dry.' That's all I remember clearly. He said that, and then he died."

Sally's face was wet. Those words—"keep your powder dry"—were what he always said to her on leaving; and now he had left her forever.

"It's all right," she said. "I'm listening. You must tell me everything. If I cry, take no notice. Go on."

"I gathered he'd dictated a letter to the servant. But I don't suppose it ever got here."

"It did," said Sally. "That was what started it all."

Bedwell rubbed his brow. Seeing that the sailor's glass was empty and that he was rapidly tiring, Frederick poured out the last of the brandy.

"Thank you. Where was I. . . . Well, the next thing that happened was that a strange pattering noise came from overhead, like big soft raindrops. Only it wasn't rain—it was bare feet running over the deck, and the next second, a great wild cry came from poor Harding at the wheel. And then a sound of smashing wood . . .

"I ran up the companionway and stopped in the shadow at the top.

"The ship was sinking. There were six or seven Chinese devils smashing in the lifeboats, and two or three of our crew stretched in their own blood on the deck. The ship was listing so much already that I saw one of those corpses start to move, almost as if it were alive, and slide down slowly into the water that was creeping up the deck to meet it. . . .

"If I live a hundred years I'll never forget the sight of that ship. It's with me still, clearer than this room; I have only to close my eyes and it's before me. . . . The sea full of light, blazing with all the colors of the rainbow, like a huge slow fireworks display—with crisp little volleys of brightness wherever anything fell into the water, and a line of trembling white fire around the edge of the ship; the still, black shape of the junk a little way off; and above us the stars—and they were all colors, too, reds and yellows and blue-whites; and the dead men in their blood on the deck, and the pirates chopping swiftly at the boats— and the sensation of sinking, falling slowly into that great bath of light. . . . I'm a slave to a terrible drug, Miss Lockhart; I've spent more days and nights in strange dreams than I care to think about; but nothing I've seen in the smoke has been stranger or more terrible than those few minutes I spent on the deck of the sinking *Lavinia.*

"And then I felt a hand tug my sleeve. I turned—and there was the servant Perak, finger to his lips.

" 'Come with me, Bedwell *tuan,*' he whispered, and I

followed, helpless as a baby. God knows how he'd done it, but he'd lowered the captain's gig, and it bobbed in the water over the stern. We got in and rowed away—just a little distance. Should I have stayed? Should I have tried to fight off the pirates, bare-handed as I was, and them with cutlasses? I don't know, Miss Lockhart; I don't know . . .

"Then the pirates left, and got into their boat and rowed off. The *Lavinia* was about to sink, and the rest of the crew—those who hadn't been cut to the deck—were struggling to free the lifeboats, and crying out with rage and fear when they saw them stove in. The next minute, the schooner went down—terribly fast, as if a great hand had thrust it into the water. There was an immense swirl, and cries from the sailors as they fell into the sea. The gig was a small boat—it'd hold seven or eight at a pinch—but we could save some of them. I turned it 'round and rowed toward them.

"But when we were still fifty yards off, the sharks came. The poor devils didn't have a chance. They were a shiftless, lazy lot, but there was no harm in 'em; and they were doomed before the voyage began . . .

"Pretty soon we were alone. The sea was strewn with bits of wreckage—splintered oars and broken spars and the like. We drifted through it all, feeling—nothing. Feeling numb. D'you know, I think I even fell asleep.

"How that night passed I've no idea; nor why my luck held, so that a Malay fishing boat picked us up the next day. We had no food and no water—we wouldn't have lasted twenty-four hours. They put us ashore at their village, and then we found our way to Singapore. And there . . ."

He stopped and rubbed his eyes wearily. But he kept

them closed and kept his hand over them. Frederick said quietly:

"Opium?"

Bedwell nodded. "I made my way to a den and lost myself in the smoke. A week, two weeks—who knows? I lost Perak, too. I lost everything. When I came to myself again I found a berth as able seaman on a London-bound steamer, and—well, you know the rest.

"But you can see now why the ship was sunk. Not by a reef or a typhoon; not for the sake of the insurance.

"This is how I see it. The word had gone out that Mr. Lockhart was aboard, searching around, making inquiries. Someone gave orders to muddle up the cargoes in Singapore so as to keep the ship in harbor for a week, while Ah Ling and his foul crew made haste to come and meet us.

"Sinking the ship was just a way of concealing your father's murder. One death on its own would look suspicious, but one among many in a shipwreck, especially if there's no body to examine—well, it looks more like an act of God.

"The two days' sailing out of Singapore I can't understand. But one thing I've learned in the East is that nothing's done without a reason; something made them hold off till the night of the thirtieth, when they could have attacked us any time before that. . . . Though I suppose it did get us clear of the shipping lanes.

"Someone organized all that. Someone powerful and ruthless; someone close to Singapore. It's my guess that the secret society I told you about was at the bottom of it. They have the most terrible penalties for their enemies, or those who betray them.

"But what they're hiding . . ."

There was a silence.

Sally got up and crossed to the fire, and put a shovelful of coal on the embers, stirring them up into a bright blaze.

"Mr. Bedwell, is it possible—when you take opium, I mean—is it possible for your memory to recall things you'd forgotten?"

"It's happened many times. As if I were living them again. But I don't need opium to remember that night the *Lavinia* went down. . . . Why d'you ask?"

"Oh . . . It was something I'd heard. But there's another thing—these secret societies. Triads, are they called?"

"That's right."

"And you said the firm's agents were members of one?"

"Rumored to be."

"Do you know which one it was?"

"I do. And that was where I'd heard the name of Ah Ling the pirate. He was said to be a headman of the same society. It was called the Fan Lin Society, Miss Lockhart. The Seven Blessings."

14

Arms and the Girl

THE NEXT MORNING SALLY WENT OUT FOR A WALK TO
think over what Matthew Bedwell had told her. It was
damp and cold, and the mist in the air seemed to dull the
sound of the traffic. She walked slowly down toward the
British Museum.

So her father had been murdered . . .

She had suspected it, of course; Bedwell's story only
confirmed her fears. But it was more difficult to unravel
now, not less: for even though the meaning of the Seven
Blessings was clear now, why should that society have
needed to become involved with a shipping firm? And
what secret did they have that was so precious that several
men's deaths were necessary to keep it hidden? Mr. Higgs
had known: did Mr. Selby? And who was this stranger,
the man from the Warwick Hotel, whose letter had so
frightened him?

And then there was her father's dying message: "Keep
your powder dry." Be prepared, that meant. Stay on
guard.

Well, she'd been doing that, and she'd carry on doing it;
but it didn't explain anything. She wished Mr. Bedwell

had remembered the other things her father had said—any little clue would have been better than nothing. Perhaps it would come back to him when he'd recovered under his brother's care. She profoundly hoped so.

She arrived at the British Museum and wandered up to the great flight of steps. Pigeons pecked among the columns; three girls a little younger than herself, under the care of a governess, climbed the steps, talking cheerfully. She, with her thoughts of sudden death and guns, did not belong in that calm and civilized place.

She turned back to Burton Street; there was something she wanted to ask Trembler.

SHE FOUND HIM in the shop, arranging a display of portrait frames. She heard Rosa's laughter from the kitchen, and Trembler told her that the Reverend Nicholas had arrived.

"I knew I'd seen him before," he said. "Two or three years ago in Sleeper's Gymnasium, it was, just when the Marquess o' Queensberry's rules come in. He made a wager with Bonny Jack Foggon, one o' the old bare-knuckle boys. They fought fifteen rounds, him with gloves on and Foggon without, and he won, though he was terrible marked."

"The other man had bare fists?"

"Aye, and that was his undoing. See, the gloves protect your hands as well as the other feller's face, and after fifteen rounds he was punching a hell of a lot harder than Foggon, in spite o' Bonny Jack pickling his fists for years. I remember the punch as laid him out—a lovely right cross, and that was the end of it, and the triumph of the Queensberry Rules. Course, Mr. Bedwell wasn't a reverend then. Did yer want something, miss?"

"Yes . . . Trembler, do you know where I can get a gun? A pistol?"

He blew through his mustache—a trick he had when he was surprised.

"Depends what sort," he said. "I suppose you mean a cheap one."

"Yes. I've only got a few pounds. And I can't really go into a gunsmith's myself—they'd probably refuse to sell me one. Could you buy one for me?"

"You know how to use a pistol, do you?"

"Yes. I had one, but it was stolen. I told you."

"So you did. Well, I'll see what I can do."

"If you'd rather not, I can ask Frederick to do it. But I thought that you might know someone . . ."

"Someone in the criminal way, you mean."

She nodded.

"Well, I might. I'll see."

The door opened, and Adelaide came in with some newly printed stereographs. Trembler's expression changed, and a huge gap-toothed smile appeared under his mustache.

"Here's my ladylove," he said. "Where you been?"

"I been with Mr. Garland," she said, and then saw Sally. "Morning, miss," she whispered.

Sally smiled and went through to join the others.

ON WEDNESDAY afternoon, two days after the stranger had got off the boat, Mrs. Holland had a visit from Mr. Selby. This was quite unexpected; she hardly knew the etiquette for the polite reception of a blackmail victim, but she did her best.

"Come in, Mr. Selby," she said, beaming yellowly. "Cup o' tea?"

"Very kind," muttered the gentleman. "Thank 'ee."

They exchanged civilities for some minutes, until Mrs. Holland began to lose her patience.

"Well, now," she said. "Out with it. I can see as you're bursting to tell me some good news."

"You're a clever woman, Mrs. Holland. I've conceived an admiration for you in the short time of our acquaintance. You've got hold of something about me—I won't deny it—"

"You can't," said Mrs. Holland.

"I wouldn't if I could. But there's richer pickings than me. You've got a hold of the edge of something. How'd you like to get your hands on the rest of it?"

"Me?" she said in mock astonishment. "I ain't the party involved, Mr. Selby. I'm just the broker. I should have to put any proposal to my gentleman."

"Well, o' course," said Mr. Selby impatiently, "the gentleman'll have to be consulted, if you insist. I don't see why you don't drop him, and deal direct yourself—but it's your decision."

"That's right," said the lady. "Well, are you going to tell me all about it?"

"Not just straight off, of course not. What d'you take me for? I got to have my guarantees, same as you."

"What d'you want, then?"

"Protection. And seventy-five percent."

"Protection you can have, seventy-five percent you can't. Forty, yes."

"Oh, give over. Forty? Sixty at least . . ."

They settled on fifty percent each, as both had known they would; and then Mr. Selby began to talk. He spoke for some time, and when he had finished, Mrs. Holland was silent, staring into the empty grate.

"Well?" he said.

"Oh, Mr. Selby. You are a one. You sound like you been caught up in something bigger than what you expected."

"No, no," he said unconvincingly. "Only I'm a bit tired o' that line now. The market's not what it was."

"And you want to get out while you're still alive, eh?"

"No, no. . . . I only thought as it might be to our advantage to join forces. Kind of a partnership."

She tapped her teeth with the toasting-fork.

"Tell you what," she said. "You do one thing for me, and I'll come in with yer."

"What?"

"Your partner, Lockhart, had a daughter. She must be—oh, sixteen, seventeen now."

"What do you know about Lockhart? Seems to me you know a bloody sight too much about everything."

She stood up.

"Good-bye, then," she said. "I'll send you my gentleman's next bill in the morning."

"No, no!" he said hastily. "I beg your pardon. I didn't mean to offend. I'm sorry, Mrs. Holland."

He was sweating, a fact she observed with interest, for it was a cold day. Pretending to be mollified, she sat down again.

"Well, seeing as it's you," she went on, "I don't mind telling you that me and the Lockharts, father and daughter, is old friends. I've known that girl for years. The only thing is, I've lost touch. You find out where she's living now, and I'll see you won't lose by it."

"But how am I going to do that?"

"That's your affair, and it's my price. That—and fifty percent."

He frowned, and growled, and twisted his gloves and thumped his hat; but he was caught. Then another thought occurred to him.

"Here," he said, "I've told you a good deal, I have. Now what about your coming clean as well? Who's this gentleman o' yours, eh? Where did you hear all that stuff in the first place?"

She peeled back her upper lip in a reptilian snarl. He flinched, and then realized that she was smiling.

"Too late to ask that now," she said. "We made the bargain already, and I don't recall as that was part of it."

All he could do was sigh. With the uneasy feeling that he had done the wrong thing, Mr. Selby got up to go, leaving Mrs. Holland smiling fondly at him like a crocodile with a new baby.

And ten minutes afterward, Mr. Berry said to her:

"Who was that gent as left just now, Mrs. Holland?"

"Why?" she said. "D'you know him?"

"No, ma'am. Only he was being watched. A thickset feller, sunburned sort of look about him, was hanging about by the cemetery. He waited till your gent left, then he made a note in a little book and follered him without being seen."

Mrs. Holland's rheumy eyes opened, and then the lids came down again.

"D'you know, Mr. Berry," she said, "this is an interesting game we're in. I wouldn't miss this for the world."

It didn't take Trembler long to find Sally a gun. The very next day, while Adelaide was helping Rosa with some sewing, he beckoned Sally into the shop and thrust a brown paper parcel across the counter.

"Cost me four pounds," he said. "And there's powder and ball as well in there."

"Powder and ball?" said Sally, dismayed. "I was hoping for something more up-to-date . . ."

She gave Trembler the money and opened the parcel. The little box-lock pistol inside was no more than six inches long, with a short stumpy barrel and a large curved hammer. The handle was oak, and fitted her hand neatly; it did not seem badly balanced. The maker's name—Stocker of Yeovil—was one she recognized, and the government proof marks were stamped under the barrel as they should be; but the top of the barrel around the nipple, where the percussion cap exploded, was deeply pitted and worn. A packet of powder, a little bag of lead bullets, and a box of percussion caps completed the armory.

"Ain't it any good?" said Trembler. "I gets very nervous around guns."

"Thank you, Trembler," she said. "I'll have to try it a few times, but it's better than nothing."

She drew back the hammer, testing the strength of the spring, and looked down the narrow metal tube where the flash of the percussion cap was led to the powder. It needed a good cleaning, and it hadn't been fired for a long time; *that barrel*, she thought, *looks distinctly frail.*

"Sooner you than me," he said. "I'm off to clean the studio; we've got a sitting this morning."

FREDERICK WAS setting up the big camera. She borrowed some of his light oil and settled herself at the kitchen table to take the gun apart. The smell of the oil, the feel of the metal under her fingers, the sensation of removing little by little all the obstructions which lay between a machine and its function, all gave her a feeling of calm, impersonal happiness. Finally it was done, and she laid it down and wiped her hands.

She would have to test it. She took a deep breath and let it out slowly. She was afraid of that corroded barrel. The mechanism was in order; the trigger moved cleanly; the hammer swept down precisely on the right spot; nothing was bent or twisted, nothing was cracked. But if the barrel could not contain the force of the explosion, she would lose her right arm.

She tilted a quantity of the black, gritty powder into the barrel and tamped it down firmly. Then she tore off a little square of blue cloth from the hem of the dress Rosa had been altering, and wrapped it around one of the balls of lead to ensure a snug fit; and then the ball joined the powder in the barrel, and a patch of wadding followed it. She rammed them down hard and then took a percussion cap from the box—a little copper cylinder with a closed end, containing a quantity of fulminate, a chemical compound which exploded when struck by the hammer. She pulled the hammer back until it had clicked twice, fitted the cap over the nipple, and then with extreme care held the hammer while she gently pulled the trigger. This let the hammer down halfway, to a position where it was locked.

Trembler and Adelaide were in the shop, Frederick was in the studio, Rosa had gone to the theater; there was no one to watch and distract her. She went out into the yard. The peeling door of the wooden shed would do as a target. Checking that there was nothing in the shed but broken flowerpots and empty sacks, she measured out ten paces from the hut and turned.

The air in the yard was chilly, and she was lightly clad. Images of a shattered arm, of blood spurting from torn flesh and splintered bone, insisted on crowding into her mind; but neither the cold nor her imagination made her shiver, and the hand she raised to aim the pistol was perfectly steady. She was satisfied.

She pulled back the hammer one extra click to unlock it, and aimed at the center of the door.

Then she squeezed the trigger.

The gun leaped in her hand, but she was expecting that and had allowed for it. The huge bang and the smell of the powder were different from those she was used to, but close enough to delight her senses, and in the same split second she realized that the barrel had held, that she still had an arm and a hand, and that everything in the yard was the same as it had been before the shot.

Including the door of the shed.

There was no bullet hole anywhere to be seen. Puzzled, she examined the pistol, but it was empty. Had she forgotten to put a ball in? No, she remembered the square of cloth from the blue dress. Then what had happened? Where had the ball gone? The door was big enough by any standards—she could have put a bullet through a visiting card at that distance.

Then she saw the hole. It was two feet to the left of the door, and a foot from the ground; she had been aiming at roughly the height of her own head. She was glad her father had not seen that shot. But surely she hadn't let the recoil destroy her aim? She rejected that idea at once. She had fired hundreds of rounds; she knew how to fire a pistol.

It must be the gun itself, she concluded. A short, wide,

unrifled barrel just did not make for accuracy. She sighed. Still, at least she now had something which would make a loud noise and smell of gunpowder, and it might serve to frighten anyone who attacked her; but she would only have one shot . . .

The kitchen door opened, and Frederick came running out.

"What the devil—" he began.

"It's all right," she said. "Nothing's broken. Did you hear the noise inside?"

"I should say we did. My fair client leaped out of the chair and almost out of the picture altogether. What *are* you doing?"

"Testing a pistol. I'm sorry."

"In the middle of London? You're a savage, Lockhart. I don't know what effect you'll have on Mrs. Holland, but by God you terrify me." Then, more kindly, he said, "That was the Duke of Wellington, talking about his soldiers. Are you all right?"

He moved closer and put a hand on her shoulder. She was trembling all over now, and felt cold and hurt and angry with herself.

"Look at you," he said. "You're shaking like a leaf. How on earth can you shoot straight if you're trembling like that? Come inside and get warm."

"I don't shake when I'm going to shoot," she muttered, unable to find her voice; and she let herself be led inside. Then she thought, *How can he be so stupid? How can he be so blind?* And simultaneously: *How can I be so feeble?*

She said nothing, and sat down to clean the pistol.

15

The Turk's Head

MRS. HOLLAND, IN PURSUANCE OF HER AGREEMENT with Mr. Selby, detailed one of her young men to look after him. This youth sat in the office picking his nails and whistling tunelessly, and went to and fro with Mr. Selby, annoying everyone they met with his insistence on searching them for hidden weapons. Jim was vastly entertained, and made the young man search him every time he came into the office—which he did as often as possible, until Mr. Selby lost his temper and ordered him out.

But tormenting Mr. Selby was only one of Jim's preoccupations. He spent a good deal of time in Wapping over the next few days. He made the acquaintance of a night watchman on the jetty by Aberdeen Wharf, who fed him information about Mrs. Holland in exchange for much-used copies of *Stirring Tales for British Lads*. The information was not very interesting, but it was something; and so were the snippets of news he gathered from the mudlarks—boys and girls who earned a living by picking up lumps of coal and other bits and pieces from the mud at low tide. They sometimes turned their attention to unguarded boats as well; anything along the shore was fair game. They knew plenty about Mrs. Holland, too, and they followed her movements with close attention; for instance, on the day after Sally tried out her new gun, they were able to tell Jim that Mrs. Holland and Mr. Berry had gone out in the morning, heading west and dressed against the cold, and that they hadn't yet returned.

The origins of that particular expedition lay in the scraps of paper Mrs. Holland had received after their detour through the hands of Ernie Blackett. At first she had thought Sally had made up the message on purpose to mislead her, but the more she looked into the words, the more there seemed to be a kind of sense in them; but she was damned if she could see what.

Finally, she lost patience.

"Come on, Mr. Berry," she said. "We're off to Swaleness."

"What for, ma'am?"

"A fortune."

"Where is it?"

"I wish I bleedin' knew."

"Then what are we going there for?"

"You know what, Jonathan Berry," she said passionately, "you're a fool. Henry Hopkins was flash and unreliable, but he wasn't a fool. I can't abide a fool."

"Sorry, ma'am," said Mr. Berry, feeling ashamed of himself without knowing why.

Mrs. Holland's plan was to visit Foreland House and interrogate Major Marchbanks's drunken housekeeper, if she was still there, in the hope that she might know something; but after a muddy walk in the biting wind, they found the place empty and locked. Mrs. Holland cursed fluently for a good ten minutes without repeating herself and then lapsed into a moody silence as they tramped back toward the town.

Halfway there, she stopped suddenly.

"Here," she said. "What's the name of that pub by the harbor?"

"Pub, ma'am? I don't recall seeing one," said Mr. Berry courteously.

"No, you wouldn't, I suppose, you pork-brained water-swiller. But if it's the Turk's Head like I think it is—"

She spoke for the first time that day without venom, and Mr. Berry felt his spirits lifting. She was scrutinizing her piece of paper again.

"Come on," she said. "D'you know, Mr. Berry, I think I got it . . ."

Stuffing the paper into her bag, she led off at a faster rate. Mr. Berry followed faithfully.

"IF I TELLS YOU to drink a mug o' beer, you'll bloody well drink it," she said much later. "I ain't having you sitting there like a bloody temperance meeting swilling lemonade, a great big man like you—why, it'd attract unwholesome attention. You do as you're told."

They stood outside the inn. It was dark, Mrs. Holland having insisted that they wait until sunset; she had spent the rest of the afternoon hanging about the harbor, where the fishing boats were rising slowly with the tide that flowed in up the creek. Mr. Berry had watched, bemused, as she spoke to one old fisherman after another—meaningless questions about lights and tides and suchlike. She was a marvel, and no error.

But he wasn't going to drink beer without a fight.

"I got me principles," he said stubbornly. "I took the

pledge, and that's good enough for me. I ain't drinking no beer."

Mrs. Holland reminded him in vivid language that he was a thief, a thug, and a murderer, and she had only to snap her fingers to have him arrested, and what she knew would hang him inside a month; but he would not budge. Finally she had to give in.

"All right," she said bitterly, "lemonade, then; and I hope that little maggot of a thing you call your conscience is satisfied. Get inside, and don't breathe a word."

With the calm joy of the righteous, Mr. Berry followed her into the Turk's Head.

"Drop o' gin for me, dear," she said to the landlord, "and a glass o' lemonade for my son, what has a delicate stomach."

The landlord brought the drinks, and while Mr. Berry sipped his lemonade, Mrs. Holland engaged the man in conversation. A handsome situation he had here, facing out to sea like he did. An old pub, was it? With an old cellar, no doubt? Yes, she'd seen the little window by the step on the way in, at ground level, and she'd had a little bet with her son that you could see the sea out of it. Was she right? Only at high tide? Well, fancy that. What a shame it was dark now—she couldn't prove it to him. A glass for the landlord? Go on; it was a cold night. Yes, pity it was dark now, and they'd be on their way in a little while. She'd like to win her bet. She could? How's that? There was a buoy in the creek—you could see it when the tide was in—and there was lights, was there, on the buoy? There, Alfred! (To Mr. Berry, who sat befuddled.) Will that prove it to yer?

Kicked, he nodded hard, and surreptitiously rubbed his ankle. "Yes, Mother," he said.

Exchanging a broad wink with Mrs. Holland, the land-lord lifted the flap of the counter and let them through.

"Down the steps," he said. "You have a squint out the winder, and you'll see it."

The cellar door was in a little passage behind the bar, and the steps were in darkness. Mrs. Holland struck a match and looked around.

"Shut the door," she hissed up to Mr. Berry.

He pushed it to and stumbled down after her.

"Careful," she said. She blew the match out, and they stood on the steps in the dark.

"What are we looking for?" he whispered.

" 'A place of darkness,' " she whispered. "That's this cellar. 'Under a knotted rope'—that's the Turk's Head."

"Eh?"

"A Turk's Head is a kind of knot. Didn't yer know that? No, o' course you wouldn't. 'Three red lights'—there's a buoy out there in the creek what flashes three times—'when the moon pulls on the water'—when the tide's in. See? It all fits. Now all we got to do is look for the light—"

"Is that it, Mrs. Holland?"

He was pointing at a small square of dim radiance in the blackness.

"Where?" she said. "I can't see nothing. Get out the way."

He moved up a step, and she took his place, peering out of the tiny window.

"That's it!" she said. "That's it! Now, quick: 'Three red lights shine clearly on the spot'—"

She turned around. By some freak, the old bull's-eye glass of one of the panes in the window acted as a lens, fo-cusing the distant flashes onto a spot in the stone wall—a spot where the stone was loose, as she discovered when she dug her urgent claws into the soft mortar it was set in.

She pulled the stone out. It was only the size of a brick; she gave it to Mr. Berry and reached inside the hole.

"There's a box," she said, her voice shaking. "Strike a match, quick. *Quick!*"

He put down the stone and did as she said, to see her drawing a little brass-studded box out of the hole in the wall.

"Hold it still, blast yer," she said, but it was her own hands she was cursing. She fumbled at the lid, trying to manipulate the catch; and then the match went out.

"Strike another," she snarled. "That bloody landlord'll be down in a minute—"

The light flared up again in his fingers. He held it close as she twisted the catch this way and that and finally forced it back.

The box was empty.

"It's gone," she said.

Her voice was quiet and shocked.

"Gone, Mrs. Holland?"

"The ruby, you great staring toad. It was here—in this box—and someone's had it."

Bitterly she thrust the box back into the hole, after checking that there was nothing else there, and jammed the stone in place just as the door opened and the light of a candle spilled down the stairs.

"All right?" came the landlord's voice.

"Yes, thank you, dear. I seen the light, and so's my son. Ain't you, Alfred?"

"Yes, Mother. I seen it all right."

"Much obliged to yer," said Mrs. Holland as they left

the cellar. "You ain't showed anyone else down there recent, I suppose?"

"Not since Major Marchbanks come down here a month or two back. He was looking at the Tudor foundations, he said. Nice old gent. Killed 'isself the other week."

"Fancy that," she said. "No one else, then?"

"My girl might have let someone down, only she's not here at the moment. Why?"

"No reason," said Mrs. Holland. "It's a quaint little place, that's all."

"It is that," he said. "All right, then?"

Mrs. Holland had to be satisfied with that. But she said to Mr. Berry as they waited for their train: "There's only one person who knew where that ruby was, and that's the girl. Hopkins is dead, and Ernie Blackett don't count. . . . It's the girl. I'll have her, Mr. Berry. I'll have her and I'll tear her open, I will. I'm angry now, and I'll have her life, you see if I don't."

16

Protecting the Property

ON FRIDAY, THE EIGHTH OF NOVEMBER, MR. SELBY TOOK a trip on the river. It was part of his job, occasionally, to make inspections of vessels in the docks, of cargoes in the warehouses, and to issue certificates and bills of lading. He had been a good shipping agent once. He was brisk and vigorous, and he was a good judge of the value of most goods both in London and in foreign markets; he had an eye for a ship, and few people had been known to get the better of him in a bargain.

So when the chance came up to inspect a schooner to replace the lost *Lavinia*, Mr. Selby took it at once—with a feeling of relief. Here was a job that didn't involve unpleasantness, that wasn't going to mix him up in anything murky or Chinese: just a straightforward shipping job. So on Friday afternoon he traveled to the Blackwall Railway Terminus, well wrapped up against the cold, and with a flask of brandy in an inside pocket to clear his judgment.

With him went Mr. Berry. The first bodyguard had had an unfortunate adventure involving a policeman, a public house, and a stolen watch, and in the absence of anyone better, Mrs. Holland had sent Mr. Berry along to Cheapside.

"Where are we going, Mr. Selby?" he said as they got off the train.

"On the river," said Mr. Selby shortly.

"Oh."

They walked to Brunswick Pier, where Mr. Selby had arranged for a boat to be ready to take them to the ship-building yards by the mouth of Bow Creek where the schooner was tied up. The pier was deserted, but for a single skiff bobbing at the foot of the steps, with a figure in a shabby green greatcoat and a large hat, holding the oars.

When they arrived, the boatman stepped out of the skiff and helped Mr. Selby down. Then he turned to Mr. Berry.

"Sorry, sir," he said. "The boat'll only take two."

"But I'm supposed to stay with him," said Mr. Berry. "I got to. I been told."

"Sorry, sir. There's no room."

"What's going on?" called Mr. Selby. "Get a move on, will yer? I'm a busy man."

"He says there's only room for two, Mr. Selby," said Jonathan Berry.

"Well, take the oars and row yerself," said Mr. Selby. "Only don't hang about."

"Very sorry, sir," said the boatman. "Company policy not to hire out a boat without an employee aboard. Nothing I can do, sir."

Mr. Selby snarled with impatience. "Oh, very well. You stay here, Wossname. Don't stir from this pier."

"All right, Mr. Selby," said his bodyguard.

He sat down on a bollard, lit a short pipe, and watched placidly as Mr. Selby was borne away on the turbid river.

And it was not until they came to close the pier at six

o'clock, and found him still sitting there, that he realized anything was wrong.

"YOU BLOODY great codfish," said Mrs. Holland, and then she treated him to an analysis of his character, a list of his ancestors, and a prognostication of his future.

"But he told me to wait hisself," protested Mr. Berry.

"You don't realize what's going on, do you? You don't realize what you done at all, do you, you great big stone?"

"Only because you won't tell me," muttered the big man, but he dared not say it loudly.

For Mrs. Holland had by now become so obsessed by the ruby that she could see nothing else. Mr. Selby had been a temporary interest, promising for a while, but with nothing like the gripping fascination of the other. She ejected the few lodgers she had so as to have the house clear, and hung a sign saying NO VACANCIES on the front door; she dispatched spies to all parts of London to look out for Sally and Adelaide, and, just in case, for a photographer with fair hair as well; she drove Mr. Berry into a state of acute nervousness, in which her least movement made him start, her least word made him jump, and her sudden appearance in a room made him leap up like a guilty schoolboy. She padded around the house muttering and cursing; she prowled around the edges of her territory, from Wapping Old Stairs to Shadwell Basin, from Hangman's Wharf to the line of the Blackwall Railway, fixing her glittering eyes on every young girl she saw; she did not sleep, but sat up in the kitchen, brewing tarlike tea and napping in snatches. Mr. Berry walked on tiptoe and spoke very politely.

* * *

As for Sally, she felt lost.

She had bought a weapon, but she didn't know her enemy; she had learned about her father's death, but she could see no reason for it.

And days were going by.... She felt that she had started something, with her first visit to the offices of Lockhart and Selby, that was now out of control. Things were revolving obscurely around her, like great dangerous machines in a darkened factory, and she was walking blindly among them . . .

She knew she could learn more: but only at the cost of another journey into the Nightmare. And she couldn't pay that; not yet.

Then there was the ruby. Clearly it had meant something important in her past, and clearly if she could find it now she'd be in possession of a fortune. "It is clearly yours by my gift, and by the laws of England," Major Marchbanks had written. But if that strange jumble of words—a place of darkness—a knotted rope—*was* a description of a hiding place, neither she nor Frederick could make any sense of it. Major Marchbanks might as well have thrown the ruby into the sea for all the chance she had of finding it.

But did she really want to find it, anyway? It was too close to the Nightmare. It was the past, and she was moving into the future; because for the first time she had friends, and a home, and a purpose. With every day that passed, she felt more secure in her knowledge of the business, and more full of ideas for developing it. Unfortunately most of them cost money, and there was no capital available. She could not use hers, because she could only get at it through Mr. Temple; and if she went to him she would lose her independence at once.

It was easier to think about Frederick. Such a mixture of lazy flippancy and passionate anger, of bohemian carelessness and dedicated perfectionism! Frederick was a topic to fascinate any psychologist. She thought: *I must ask him to teach me photography. But later, not yet; not until I'm free of this mystery.*

With an effort, she turned her mind back to the darkness—back to Mrs. Holland. So the young woman and the old one each found their thoughts occupied by the other; and when that happens to people, sooner or later they meet.

EARLY ON Saturday morning, a man and a boy in a barge laden with horse manure spotted a body in the water in that part of the river known as Erith Reach. With the aid of a boat hook they got it on board, and laid it ceremoniously on top of their floating dunghill. It was the boy's first corpse, and he was very pleased with it. He wanted to keep it for a while, and display it for the admiration of the passing traffic; but his father put the boat in at Purfleet and gave the remains to the local magistrates. The horse manure went on to the farms of Essex.

JIM HAD TAKEN to spending most of the weekend at Burton Street. Rosa had commandeered him at once for the Stereographic Repertory Company. He was Oliver Twist; he was a Boy Standing on the Burning Deck; he was Puck; he was a Prince in the Tower, with Frederick as an unconvincing Wicked Uncle. But no matter how he was costumed or how noble the role, his features were so formed that the only expression the camera could catch on them was a cheerful villainy. They tried him once with

"When Did You Last See Your Father?" and he looked, said Frederick, as if he were persuading the Parliamentarians that he could let them have a nice lot of secondhand muskets, dirt cheap.

"Here," he said to Rosa when he came in on Saturday, "old Selby's missing! He never come in this morning. I bet he's done in. I bet that geezer from the Warwick Hotel's cut his throat."

"Stand still," said Rosa, her mouth full of pins. The studio had been transformed into Palestine, with the aid of a painted backcloth, and she was trying to make Jim look like the boy David for a Biblical series that Trembler said they could sell to missionary societies. "When did you last wash your knees?"

"I bet he never washed his bloody knees, neither. Who's going to look at this picture, anyway?"

"Cannibals," said Sally.

"Well, it'll come off in the pot, won't it? You don't seem to care about old Selby. I bet he's dead."

"Quite possibly," said Rosa. "Now, will you stop jigging about, for goodness' sake. We've got loads of work to do . . ."

A customer came into the shop, and Sally went to serve him. When she came back she could hardly stop smiling.

"Listen!" she said. "Listen, this is marvelous! That was a man from Chainey's, the printers. They want to print lots of our pictures and put them on sale all over London. Already! What d'you think of that?"

"First-rate!" said Frederick. "Which ones?"

"How much are they going to pay?" said Rosa.

"I told him to come back on Monday. I said we were too busy to discuss it at the moment, but we'd had offers from several other firms and we'd have to weigh them all up. When they come back—"

"You didn't!" said Rosa. "But that's not true!"

"Well, perhaps not yet. But we will. I'm just anticipating a little to put the price up. Frederick, when they come back, you must deal with them. I'll tell you what to say."

"I hope you will. I wouldn't have the least idea. Oh! Have you seen this? I meant to show you earlier."

He folded back a copy of *The Times*.

"For heaven's sake," said Rosa crossly. "Are you going to take any pictures today, or not?"

"Of course I am," he said, "but this might be important. Listen: 'Miss Sally Lockhart. If Miss Sally Lockhart, daughter of the late Matthew Lockhart, Esquire, of London and Singapore, will enquire for Mr. Reynolds at the Warwick Hotel, Cavendish Place, she will learn something to her advantage.' What d'you think of that?"

Jim whistled. "That's him," he said. "That's the bloke what killed Selby."

"It's a trick," said Sally. "I'm not going."

"Shall I go, and pretend to be you?" said Rosa.

"Don't go," said Jim. "He'll cut your throat, same as he did old Selby's."

"What do you know about Selby?" said Frederick. "You're obsessed, you horrible little boy."

"Betcher," said Jim at once. "Betcher half a crown he's dead."

"Done," said Frederick. "Sally, I'll come with you if you like. He couldn't do anything if I was there."

"Supposing it's Mr. Temple, though?" she said. "You keep forgetting that I'm supposed to be hiding. He's legally responsible for me so he's bound to be trying all kinds of ways to find me again."

"But it might be something to do with your father,"
said Rosa. "He's called you Sally and not Veronica, for a
start."

"That's true. Oh, I don't know what to do. But . . . oh, I
don't know. There's too much to do here. Let's get on
with this picture. . . ."

ON SUNDAY AFTERNOON, Adelaide and Trembler went
for a walk. They went past the British Museum, down the
Charing Cross Road, and looked at Nelson on his column;
then they strolled along the Mall, and went to pay a call
on Her Majesty the Queen, only she wasn't in, for the
Royal Standard wasn't flying over Buckingham Palace.

"She must be at Windsor," said Trembler. "Just like
her. Let's have some hot chestnuts instead."

So they bought some chestnuts and walked through the
park, and saved some bits to give to the ducks, who came
and fought for them like little battleships. Adelaide had
never dreamed of an afternoon like this. She laughed and
joked with Trembler as if she'd forgotten how to be unhappy, and he laughed, too, and taught her how to skim
stones across the water, until a park keeper came and told
them off. Then when his back was turned Trembler stuck
out his tongue, and they both burst out laughing again.

Which was when they were spotted.

A young worker from the sawmill behind Wapping
High Street was out walking with his best girl, a housemaid from Fulham. He had had dealings of a mildly criminal nature (tobacco extracted from a warehouse) with
one of Mrs. Holland's lodgers, and remembered that that
lady was offering a reward for news of Adelaide's whereabouts. He was a sharp-eyed young man, and he recognized her at once. He steered the best girl away from the

path they were treading and began to follow Adelaide and Trembler.

"Here," said the housemaid. "Wotcher doing?"

"Just act natural," said the young man. "I got me reasons."

"I know your sort o' reasons," said the housemaid. "I ain't going in no bushes with *you*. Not bloody likely!"

"Cheerio, then," he said, and left her astonished on the footpath.

He followed them out of the park and up through Trafalgar Square. He lost them at the bottom of St. Martin's Lane, and then nearly ran into them in Cecil Court, where they were gazing into the window of a toy shop. He kept up with them as far as the British Museum; nearly lost them in Coptic Street; tried to stay farther back and out of sight, because the crowds were thinner up here, and then had to get closer, because it was getting dark; and finally saw them turn the corner of Burton Street. When he got there, they had vanished—but the door of a photographer's shop was closing.

Well, that's something anyway, he thought, and hurried off back to Wapping.

17

King James's Stairs

THE MAN FROM CHAINEY'S THE PRINTERS CAME ON
Monday, as Sally had arranged. Frederick, well-
rehearsed, insisted on a royalty of twenty percent, rising
to twenty-five percent after ten thousand copies had been
sold. The printer was taken aback by this; he had expected to make a single payment and buy the pictures
outright. But Sally had thought of that and told Frederick
not to budge. The printer agreed to take the Historical series, the Famous Murders, and the Scenes from Shake-
speare. He also agreed that the pictures should be known
as Garland's, and not Chainey's; that they should be sold
at a price of two shillings and sixpence a set; and that
they, the printers, should bear the cost of the advertising.

Slightly bemused, the printer left—but not before he
had signed an agreement. Frederick rubbed his eyes, unable to believe what he'd done.

"That was just right!" said Sally. "I was listening. You
were firm and you knew just what to say. We've started!
We're on our way!"

"I'm a mass of nerves," said Frederick. "My soul is too
fine for this commercial jousting. Why don't you do it?"

"I shall, as soon as I'm old enough to be taken seriously."

"*I* take you seriously."

She looked at him. They were alone in the shop; the others had gone out for various things. He was sitting on the counter; she was standing a yard or so away, with her hands on the wooden rack Trembler had made to hold the stereographs. And she was suddenly very conscious of all this. She looked down.

"As a businesswoman?" she said, trying to keep her voice light.

"As all kinds of things. Sally, I—"

The door opened and a customer came in. Frederick jumped down from the counter and served him, while Sally went through into the kitchen. Her heart was beating fast. What she felt for Frederick was so confused and powerful that she couldn't begin to articulate it; she hardly dared think what he had been going to say. Perhaps, in another minute or two, she would have found out.

But then there was a bang on the kitchen door, and in strolled Jim.

"Jim!" she said. "What are you doing here? Aren't you at work?"

"I came to collect me winnings," he said. "Remember I made a bet with the guvnor? Well, I was right. Old Selby's dead!"

"What?"

Frederick came in at that point and stopped short.

"What are you doing here, gargoyle?" he said.

"I come to tell you some news. You owe me half a crown, for a start. Old Selby's snuffed it. They fished him out the river on Saturday and we had a copper 'round this morning, and the place is closed. There's investigations going on. So let's have me money."

Frederick threw him a coin and sat down.

"What do they know about it?" he said.

"He went off on Friday to look at a schooner near Bow Creek somewhere. He took a skiff at Brunswick Pier, and it never come back. Nor did the boatman. That big feller o' Mrs. Holland's was with him up till the pier, but he never went on the skiff, 'cause there's a witness as saw him waiting. What d'you think of that, then?"

"Blimey," said Frederick. "And you think it was the man from the Warwick Hotel?"

"Course it was. Stands to reason."

"And did you tell the police that?"

"What for?" said Jim scornfully. "Let 'em whistle."

"Jim, this is murder."

"Selby was a villain," said Jim. "He sent her dad to his death, remember? He don't deserve no better. That ain't murder—that's natural justice."

They both looked at Sally. She felt that if she said yes, we'll go to the police, the other two would agree. But a part of her mind insisted that if they did, she would never learn the truth.

"No," she said. "Not yet."

"This is dangerous," said Frederick.

"To me, not you."

"That's why I'm concerned," he retorted angrily.

"You don't understand. And I can't explain. Oh, please, Frederick, let me find my own way through this!"

He shrugged. "What d'you think, Jim?"

"She's mad. Best leave her be, in case it's catching."

"All right. But Sally, will you promise always to let me know what you're going to do, and where you are? If you're determined to thrust yourself into danger, I want to know about it."

"All right. I promise."

"Well, that's something anyway. Jim, what are you going to do today?"

"Dunno. Hang about and annoy people, I expect."

"D'you want to see how to set up the camera and take a photograph?"

"Yes, please!"

"Come on, then . . ."

They went into the studio and left Sally to herself. She turned to the newspaper, intending to look at the financial news. But her eye was caught by a headline; she started to read; and within a minute she was on her feet, white and trembling.

MYSTERIOUS ATTACK ON CLERGYMAN

_____

OXFORD BROTHERS IN MURDER MYSTERY

_____

An extraordinary series of events took place in Oxford on Saturday last, culminating in the murder of the brother of a local clergyman.

The murdered man, Mr. Matthew Bedwell, was staying with his twin brother, the Reverend Nicholas Bedwell, Curate of St. John's, Summertown.

The events began with a vicious and unprovoked attack on the Reverend Bedwell as he visited an elderly parishioner. Entering the lane which led to the invalid's cottage, the curate was set upon by a well-built man wielding a dagger.

Despite injuries to his arms and face, the Reverend Bedwell managed to fight off the assailant, who promptly vanished. Mr. Bedwell repaired to a doctor, but meanwhile, a message had arrived at the vicarage, requesting his brother to meet him by the river in Port Meadow nearby.

Thus lured out, Mr. Matthew Bedwell left the vicarage at three o'clock, and was never again seen alive. Shortly after seven in the evening, a waterman found his body in the river. His throat had been cut.

The victim of this desperate murder was a sailor, and had recently returned from a voyage to the East Indies. He and his brother were identical twins, and it is thought that this fact may explain the earlier attack upon the Reverend Bedwell; but the circumstances remain obscure.

Sally put down the paper and ran to find Frederick.

THEY WROTE at once to Nicholas Bedwell and spent the rest of the day working quietly. No one had much to say, not even Jim. Rosa left for the theater earlier than usual.

Jim had made himself so useful that they asked him to stay for supper. He went out with Trembler and Adelaide to the Duke of Cumberland, the public house around the corner, for some beer to have with the meal. Sally was cooking; they were going to have kedgeree, which was one of the only two things she knew how to cook.

Frederick had just come in from the laboratory, and Sally was preparing to lay the table, when the kitchen door flew open and Jim ran in.

"Mrs. Holland!" he gasped, out of breath. "She's got Adelaide—she was hiding 'round the corner—she grabbed her and jumped into a cab—we couldn't stop her—"

"Where's Trembler?" said Frederick, dropping the knives and forks and reaching for his coat.

"The big man knocked him down," said Jim. "It was dark—we was just coming 'round the corner there by the pub, where it's in shadder—we couldn't see nothing! She suddenly come out the alley and grabbed her, and Trembler dropped the beer and grabbed her other arm, and the big bloke took a swing at him and flattened him— he's still there as far's I know—I saw 'em shove her into a cab and it set off at a hell of a lick—"

"Sally, stay here," said Frederick. "Don't go out, don't answer the door, don't let anyone in."

"But—" she cried, too late; for he had gone, and Jim had gone with him. "But what about Trembler?" she said to the empty kitchen. She looked at the steaming kedgeree, just ready to be eaten, and felt tears of frustration come to her eyes. *Why should I stay here?* she thought angrily; *isn't it my affair?*

She flung herself into the big chair and chewed her lip. What she might have done next she didn't know; but there was a rattle as the door handle turned, and she looked up startled to see Trembler, shaking and white-faced and bleeding from a cut on the cheek. She jumped up and helped him in and sat him in the armchair.

"What happened?" she said. "Jim came running and said Mrs. Holland had—"

"They got her, the bastards," he said. He was earning his name now: shaking more than her at her worst. "They grabbed hold of her, poor little scrap, and snatched her up into a bloody cab—and I couldn't even stop 'em—that big bugger hit me and I fell over. . . . I tried, miss, God's truth I tried—but he was so big . . ."

"Fred and Jim have gone out after them," she said,

wringing out a cloth and holding it to his face. "They'll get her, don't you worry. Fred won't let anything happen to her. She'll be safe back here within an hour."

"Gawd, miss, I hope you're right. It's my fault. I didn't ought to have let her come. She's a lovely little thing . . ."

"Hush, don't blame yourself. Of course it wasn't your fault. It wasn't anyone's. Look—supper's ready, and there's no one to eat it but us. Are you going to have some?"

"I dunno if I can. I ain't hungry anymore."

Nor was Sally; but she made him have some, and ate some herself. Neither spoke until they had finished. Then he pushed his plate away and said, "Very tasty. Very nice." It had only taken them five minutes to eat.

"How's your cheek?" she said.

His eye was closing. "Bloody useless, I am," he muttered as she dabbed at it gently with a damp piece of flannel. "Can't do anything right."

"Don't be silly," she said. "This place would fall to pieces without you, and you know it. So stop feeling sorry for yourself."

She put down the flannel and suddenly found herself in the grip of an idea. She had to sit down: she had begun to tremble.

"What is it?" said the little man.

"Trembler, will you do something for me?"

"What?"

"I—" She didn't know how to put it. "Trembler, you know what happened when I went to the opium den with Fred?"

"Yes. You told us. Why? You ain't planning on going there again?"

"No. I don't have to. I've got some opium here. . . .

When Reverend Bedwell asked me to get some, I—well, I put a bit aside. I knew I'd have to go through it again. I've been steeling myself. I won't know how Mrs. Holland comes into it unless I do. I'll have to bring on my Nightmare, you see. I was going to put it off and put it off and hope she just went away, but she hasn't. And it's all coming to a head and . . . I want to do it now. Will you stay with me?"

"What—you're going to smoke the stuff here?"

"It's the only way I'll ever find the truth. Please, Trembler. Will you stay here and look after me?"

He swallowed hard. "Course I will, miss. But supposing it goes wrong? What'll I do?"

"I don't know. I trust you, Trembler. Just . . . hold me, perhaps."

"All right, miss. I'll do it."

She jumped up and kissed him, and then ran to the cupboard in the corner. The opium was wrapped in a piece of paper behind the Toby jug on the top shelf, and she had to stand on a chair to get it. She had kept a piece about the size of the tip of her little finger, and she had no idea whether that was too much, or not enough, nor how to smoke it in the first place, since she didn't have a pipe . . .

She sat at the table and pushed the plates aside. Trembler drew up a chair and sat opposite her, moving the lamp so that it shone clearly on the red oilcloth. The fire was banked up and the kitchen was warm; but to make it more secure she locked the door. Then she unwrapped the opium.

"Last time," she said, "I just happened to breathe in the fumes from someone else's pipe. Perhaps there's no need for me to actually smoke it. . . . If I just set light to it and breathe the fumes, like I did before. . . . Or maybe I ought to make sure. This is all I've got. What do you think?"

He shook his head. "I dunno, miss," he said. "My mum used to give me laudanum for the toothache when I was a boy. But that's all I know about it. They smoke it like to-bacco, do they?"

"I don't think so. The people I saw at Madame Chang's were all lying on beds, and a servant was holding the pipe for them. And lighting the opium. Perhaps they couldn't hold it for themselves. If I put it on a plate . . ."

She jumped up and brought an enameled plate to the table, and then took the box of matches from the shelf over the fire.

"I'll just hold the match to it," she said. "Then if I fall asleep or something, the match will drop on the plate and it won't matter."

She took a clean fork and pierced the sticky little ball of resin, and then held it over the plate.

"Here goes," she said.

She struck a match and held it to the opium. Her hands were perfectly steady, she saw. The flame curled up around the drug, blackening the surface; and then it began to fume and bubble. She leaned forward and breathed in deeply, and was instantly overcome with dizziness. She blinked and shook her head, and felt sick, and then the match went out.

She dropped it on the plate and reached for another.

"All right, miss?" said Trembler.

"Could you light the match for me and hold it under the opium?"

"Righto. Are you sure you want to go ahead with it?"

"Yes. I've got to. Just keep lighting matches—keep it smoking."

He struck a match and held it in place. She leaned forward, resting her arms on the table and pulling back her hair so that it wouldn't catch fire, and then breathed in deeply. The smoke tasted sweet, she thought, and bitter at the same time; and then the Nightmare began.

WAPPING IN those days was very like an island. On one side was the river, and on the other side were the docks and their entrances. To get into Wapping, therefore, you had to cross a bridge—and they were not solid, imposing structures like London Bridge, made of stone or brick, but lighter ones of iron and wood. And they all moved: they were swingbridges, or hydraulic bridges, and from time to time they swung aside or elevated themselves out of the way of the ships moving in and out of the docks. There were seven of these bridges: seven ways in, and seven ways out. It was an easy matter to put a man by each of them. There were plenty of people who owed Mrs. Holland favors, and plenty more who were frightened of her.

Frederick's cab, with Jim clinging excitedly to the apron, rattled across the swingbridge over Wapping Entrance, the channel that led into the larger of the two London docks. Neither Frederick nor Jim noticed the two men by the winch on the right-hand side.

"Where to, guv?" the cabman shouted down.

"Stop here," called Frederick. "This'll do—we'll walk the rest."

They paid the driver, and the cab turned and drove back the way it had come. Frederick wished that he had more money with him, so as to keep the cab waiting there, but he had only just enough to pay for the fare as it was.

"What are we going to do?" said Jim. "I know where her house is. I been spying."

"I'm not sure," said Frederick. "Let's go and see what's happening. . . ."

They hurried along Wapping High Street, between the high, dark warehouses and the overhanging gantries and pulleys that swung above them like the equipment for some multiple execution. After a minute or two they were at the corner of Hangman's Wharf, and then Frederick held out his hand to stop them.

"Wait," he said.

He looked around the corner and tugged urgently at Jim's arm.

"Look!" he whispered. "Just in time—they're just arriving—she's getting out of the cab, and she's got Adelaide with her—"

"What are we going to do?" whispered Jim.

"Come on! Let's just grab her and run!"

Frederick leaped forward, and Jim followed at once. It was only a matter of twenty yards or so to the entrance of Holland's Lodgings, and Frederick ran lightly. Mrs. Holland was still fumbling with her keys when he reached her.

"Adelaide!" he cried, and Mrs. Holland turned in a flash. "Run! Go with Jim!"

Jim hurtled up, full pelt, and seized her hand. He tried to drag her away, but she hung back, paralyzed.

"Come *on!*" he cried, and pulled harder, and finally she went. They ran for the corner of the street and vanished—and then Frederick saw why Mrs. Holland had not moved, and why she was smiling at him; for standing right behind him, holding a short stick, was the big man, Jonathan Berry. Frederick looked around—but he was trapped. There was no way out.

THE CORNER Jim had turned was not one Adelaide would have chosen: it led them into a blind alley. But she was dazed by panic and went where he pulled her.

The place was called Church Court. It was curved, so Jim could not see the closed end, and in any case it was nearly in total darkness. When he got to the end he stumbled over a heap of refuse, ran his hands up the dark brickwork, and cursed.

"Where are we?" he said. "What's over this wall?"

"A church," she whispered. "Is she coming? Is she coming?"

"The guvnor'll hold her off. Let's get over this bloody wall . . ."

He cast around in the dimness. The wall was not high—six feet or so—but it was surmounted by spikes; he could see them in the dim light from the church windows, now that his eyes were accustomed to the gloom. He heard the sound of singing, and wondered whether a church service would be a good place to hide.

But they would have to get over the wall first. There was a barrel on its side in a corner; he rolled it to the wall and heaved it upright, and then had to go and shake Adelaide, who was crouched on the ground, whispering to herself.

"Come on, stupid," he said. "Get up here. We got to climb over the wall . . ."

"I can't," she said.

"Oh, get up, for Gawd's sake. Get up!"

He pulled her up and made her stand on the barrel. She

was trembling like a nervous rabbit, and he went on more gently, "If we get over here, we can get away and go back to Burton Street. See Trembler. But you gotta try, all right?"

He gripped the top of the wall and pulled himself up. The brickwork was thick, so there was plenty of room to stand once he had lifted himself carefully over the spikes; then he turned and leaned over to help her.

"Tuck yer skirt up so's it won't catch," he said, and shakily she did so. Then she reached up and gave him her hands, and he lifted her up. She was hardly any weight at all.

Another second, and they were down in the graveyard. Dark leaning stones, rank grass, twisted railings spread out all around them, and the great bulk of the church loomed in front. The organ was playing; it looked warm in there, and friendly, and Jim was sorely tempted. They picked their way through the graves and around to the front, where a gaslight on a bracket showed him how filthy they were.

"Put yer skirt down now," he said. "You look ridicklus."

She did as he said. He looked to the left and right; the street was empty.

"Best not go back the same way, I reckon," he went on. "It's only a step from her place, that bridge. Can we get through these bloody docks any other way?"

"By the Tobacco Dock there's a bridge," she whispered. "Up Old Gravel Lane."

"Come on, then. You show me the way. Keep in the shadder, though."

She led him around the front of the church and then off to the right, past a disused workhouse. These streets were

narrower than the High Street, and edged with small ter-
raced cottages rather than wharves and warehouses.
There were few people about; they passed a public house,
but even that was quiet, although lights blazed behind the
steamy windows.

They walked quickly onward, and Jim's hopes rose.
They'd have to walk back to Burton Street, but that
didn't matter; an hour and a half's trudging wouldn't
hurt. It had gone very well, all things considered.

They paused at the corner of Old Gravel Lane, which
was wider and better lit than the little street they were
turning out of. It was starting to rain; Jim squinted ahead,
his hand over his eyes, and saw the bulk of two or three
tall warehouses at the end of the street, and then a bridge.

"Is that it?" he said.

"Yus," she said. "That's the Tobacco Dock."

Carefully, they went around the corner and set off toward the bridge. A cart trundled past, with a tarpaulin
spread over the load, but it was gone before Jim could call
to the driver and beg a lift. One or two passers-by looked
curiously at the pair of them—the frightened little girl in
a cloak too big for her, and the boy without coat or hat on
this wet night—but most went on their way, heads down
against the weather.

They were almost at the bridge before they were spotted.

There was a night watchman's hut on the right-hand
side of the road, in front of which a fire was glowing in a
brazier, hissing and spitting at the occasional raindrop
which eluded the canvas awning hung roughly above it. A
man—two men—sat in the hut, and out of the corner of
his eye Jim saw them stand when he and Adelaide were

approaching; and he just had time to think *What are they doing that for?* when he heard one of them say:

"Come on—that's her! That's the one!"

He felt Adelaide shrink away beside him, paralyzed again. He grabbed her hand as the men came out of the hut, and they turned and shot back the way they'd come. There were no side turnings: the walls of the warehouses rose sheer and dark on either side.

"Run, for Gawd's sake! Run, Adelaide!" he cried.

He saw an opening on the left and flung himself into it, dragging her after him; and then around a left-hand corner, and then a right, until the men were out of sight.

"Where to?" he said, panting. "Come on, quick—I can hear 'em."

"Shadwell Way," she gasped. "Oh, Jim, they're going to kill me—I'm going to die, Jim—"

"Shut up and don't be stupid. They ain't going to kill yer. No one's going to kill yer. She only said that to frighten yer, the ugly old bitch. She wants Sally, not you. Come on, how do we get to Shadwell?"

They were in a little place called Pearl Street—hardly wider than an alley. She looked to the left and right, indecisively.

"There they are!" came a cry from behind them, and pounding footsteps echoed from the walls.

Once again they fled. But Adelaide was tiring, and Jim was short of breath; another corner, and another, and another, and still those heavy footsteps followed them.

In desperation Jim flung himself down a little court so narrow he could hardly squeeze through, thrusting Adelaide ahead of him. She tripped. He fell on top of her, and gasped, and lay still.

Something moved in the passage ahead of them—a quick, scuttling sound like a rat. Adelaide flinched and pressed her face into his neck.

"Hello, matey," came a voice from the darkness.

Jim looked up. A match flared, and then Jim felt his face grinning for him, of its own accord.

"Thank Gawd!" he said. "Adelaide, it's all right! This is me mate Paddy!"

Adelaide had no breath left to speak with, and she was at such an extremity of fear that she could hardly move. She looked up and saw the face of a dirty, foxy boy of about Jim's age, clad apparently in sacking. She could say nothing, so she lowered her head again onto the wet stone.

"This the gel what Mrs. Holland wants?" he said.

"You heard, have yer?" said Jim. "We got to get out o' Wapping. But she's got blokes on the bridges."

"You come to the right feller," said the boy. "I knows everything hereabouts. Everything there is to know, I knows it."

Paddy was the leader of a gang of mudlarks. He had made Jim's acquaintance when he and his pals had made the mistake of first stoning him and then meeting his answering fusillade with insults; Jim's aim was better, and his vocabulary was far richer than anything they could muster, and he earned their respect at once.

"But what are yer doing up this way?" whispered Jim. "I thought you never left the riverbank?"

"Plans, matey. I got me eye on a collier in the Old Basin. Lucky for you, eh? Can yer swim?"

"No. Can you swim, Adelaide?"

She shook her head. She was still lying prone, her face to the wall. The passage they were in was roofed over, so they were out of the rain which was beating heavily on the street behind them, but a chilly stream was running down the passage from the gutter and soaking Adelaide's dress. Barefoot Paddy took no notice.

"Tide's on the turn," he said. "Let's be goin'."

"Come on," said Jim, tugging Adelaide up. They followed Paddy farther into the passage, feeling their way in the darkness.

"Where's this?" whispered Jim.

"Animal Charcoal Works," came the reply from ahead. "There's a door just up here."

He stopped. Jim heard a key turning in a lock, and then the door creaked open.

The room they entered was cavernous and long, and the guttering flame of a candle lit only a corner of it. A dozen or more children, clad in rags, lay asleep on piles of sacking, while a wild-eyed girl a little older than Paddy held the candle. A foul, thick smell filled the air.

"Evening, Alice," said Paddy. "Two visitors."

She stared at them silently. Adelaide clung to Jim, who stared back, not at all abashed.

"We got to get 'em out o' Wapping," said Paddy. "Is Dermot on the barge?"

Alice shook her head.

"Send Charlie along to tell 'im then. You know what I mean."

She nodded at a small boy, who left at once.

"D'you live here?" said Jim.

"Aye. We keeps the rats down for rent, and sells 'em to the Fox and Goose for rattin'."

Jim looked around and saw a pile of animal bones in a corner, with something stirring on them. The something pounced, and became a boy of five or six, nearly naked, who tottered to Alice with a squirming, lashing rat in his hands. She took it without a word and thrust it into a cage.

"You can stay here if you like," said Paddy. "Handsome doss, this."

"No, we got to move. Come on, Adelaide."

Jim tugged her hand. He was worried: she was so passive, so still. He'd have liked to see a bit of fight in her.

"This way, then," said Paddy, and led them through into an even larger, even fouler-smelling room. "Got to be careful here. We ain't s'posed to have a key. They keeps the furnaces going all night, so there's a watchman somewhere."

They passed through a succession of rooms and passages, pausing occasionally to listen for footsteps, but hearing none. Eventually they reached a cellar, in one corner of which was the bottom of a chute down which bones and horns and hooves were evidently tipped: it was slippery with fat and rancid with dried blood.

"How we supposed to get up that?" said Jim.

"What's the matter with it?" said Paddy. "Tasty."

He gave his candle to Adelaide and showed them how to climb the chute by bracing themselves against the sides. Jim took the candle and shoved Adelaide up, taking no notice of her protests, and after a minute they stood at the top in the fresh air and the rain. They were in a cobbled yard with a wire fence, opening onto an alley behind a public house.

Paddy tiptoed to the fence and looked through.

"All clear," he said.

Obstacles did not seem to exist for him. The wire fence looked solid and fixed, but he knew a spot where a staple had come out of the post, and where it could be lifted aside. He held it for the other two and they stepped through swiftly.

"Fox and Goose Yard," said Paddy. "The landlord here has our rats what we catch. We got to get across Wapping Wall now, and then we're at the river. 'S only a short step."

Wapping Wall was a street, not a wall, and took only a moment to cross; and almost opposite them was the entrance to King James's Stairs. Jim could see a tangle of masts and rigging and a gleam of water.

"We can get hold of a skiff down there," said Paddy. "Easy. Row yer home. You go down—I'll keep an eye open up here."

Jim and Adelaide moved down the dark passage between the buildings and found themselves on a narrow little wharf. Beneath them, vessels lay sideways on the mud; ropes ran up from them to bollards on the wharf, and the flight of stone steps led straight down onto the foreshore.

"Where do we go, Paddy?" said Jim, and turned—and then stopped.

Mrs. Holland stood in the entrance. Paddy stood beside her.

JIM REACHED for Adelaide and put his arms around her. His mind was racing. He could find only one word to say, and he said it to Paddy.

"Why?"

"Money, mate," was the reply. "Gotta live."

"There's a good boy," said Mrs. Holland.

"I'll be back," said Jim. "I'll be back, and I'll find yer."

"You do that," said Paddy, pocketing the coin Mrs. Holland gave him. Then he vanished.

"Well, now," said Mrs. Holland. "Seems like I got yer, yer little bitch. You can't run away now, 'cause Mr. Berry's down there at the bottom o' the steps, and he'll twist yer head off. He does that with chickens, to keep his hand in. They runs around flapping their wings for a good five minutes after their heads is off. I made a little bet with him on how long you'd run about for, and he's awful keen to win it, so I wouldn't go down there if I was you. You're caught now, Adelaide. I got yer."

Jim could feel the child making little convulsive movements as he held her.

"What d'you want her for?" he said, and then he felt cold, because Mrs. Holland looked directly at him for the first time, and he knew that she really was capable of having a child's head pulled to see if she'd run about. She was capable of anything.

"I want to punish her for running away. I want all kinds of things out o' that child. Yes, come on up, Mr. Berry."

Jim turned and saw the big man climbing the steps. The little light there was didn't reach his face, so he seemed to have no face at all, to be all shapeless malevolence. Adelaide pressed herself into Jim's side, and he looked around desperately for a way of escape, but there was none.

"It's Miss Lockhart you want, not Adelaide," he said. "You wants the ruby, don't yer? Well, Adelaide don't bloody know where it is. Let her go."

The only light on the sodden waterfront was the dim gleam from a distant window; but for a second, another light seemed to shine out of Mrs. Holland's eyes as she looked past Jim at Mr. Berry. Jim turned and saw the big man raising his stick. He pushed Adelaide behind him.

"You try it, mate," he said, staring up at Mr. Berry with all the daring he possessed.

The stick crashed down. Jim raised his arm and caught the whole force of it on his elbow. He nearly fainted. He heard Adelaide cry out and saw the stick raised again; and then he lowered his head and charged.

Mr. Berry brushed him aside like a fly and dealt him another blow with the terrible stick—on the shoulder this time. Jim fell into waves of pain and hardly knew he had fallen.

He tasted blood and heard a child's cry. He knew he had to help her; that was why he'd come. He forced his head around and found he couldn't get up; his arms wouldn't obey him. He struggled against the pain and found himself crying, to his deep shame and disgust. Adelaide was clinging to him, to his jacket, to his hand, to his hair—she was gripping him tight and he couldn't lift his arms to help her—Mr. Berry was holding her around the neck with one hand and tearing her loose from Jim with the other; she was choking, she was gasping, her eyes were rolling—the big man was growling like a bear; his lips were drawn back from his broken teeth, his red eyes glowed closer and closer, he had her loose, he lifted her higher—

"Put her down," said Frederick Garland. "Put her down at once or I'll kill you."

Mr. Berry stood still. Jim wrenched his head around. Frederick was standing limply, one hand against the wall. His face was terribly marked. An eye was closed, his mouth was swollen, one cheek was blackened and cut, and he was shaking all over. Mrs. Holland stood and watched comfortably.

"How?" said Mr. Berry.

"Put her down and find out," said Frederick.

"I thought I sorted you out," said Mr. Berry.

"You're losing your touch, Mr. Berry," said Mrs. Holland. "Mind you, he's a game chicken, this one. That makes four times now he's crossed my path. I want him dead, Mr. Berry. Give me the girl."

Adelaide was as limp as a doll. Mr. Berry dropped her and Mrs. Holland seized her at once.

"He'll kill yer, Fred," croaked Jim.

"No, he won't," said Frederick thickly.

Then Mr. Berry ran at him, and Frederick dodged. Jim thought: *Never, never—he'll never live. But he's brave, though.*

Frederick took a blow to the head and fell, but twisted out of reach of Mr. Berry's boots. *He ain't got his stick,* thought Jim; *he must've dropped it to pick Adelaide up.* And then Frederick reached the wall and pushed sideways, sweeping his leg around to bring the big man down.

He fell like a tree, and Frederick was on him at once, pummeling and punching and gouging and twisting—but he was so slight and so weakened that his blows were like those of a child. Mr. Berry brought up an arm like an oak beam and swept Frederick aside. Jim struggled frantically to get up, and put his weight on the damaged arm for a moment, only to find it collapsing the wrong way under him. He crumpled at once into such a blaze of pain as he had never imagined. His head struck something loose as he fell. *The stick,* he thought, and fainted.

Another second and he was awake again, to find Frederick on his knees a yard away, shielding himself from a barrage of blows that thundered down on his shoulders and head. He struck out in reply and missed with three blows for every one that landed—but he was so weak now that his punches would hardly have hurt Adelaide. Jim twisted and reached out with his good arm till it found the stick. *I'm going to die of this pain,* he thought. *I can't bear it—but look at Fred—he won't stop—nothing'll stop him, he's like me, he is—he's a good un—*

"Here y'are, Fred," he said, and thrust the stick at him. Frederick felt it in his hands before Mr. Berry saw what was happening, and the feel of it seemed to give him strength. He put both hands around it and jabbed it forward into the big man's stomach. Mr. Berry gasped, and Frederick did it again and scrambled to his feet.

They were a yard or so from the edge of the wharf. Frederick knew this was his last chance. Some ghostly remnant of his fencing came back, and he balanced himself and lashed forward. He could hardly see: both eyes were filled with blood; but he felt the stick connect, and heard Jim's cry—"This way! This way, Fred!"

He struck again and wiped his eyes. Jim hurled himself at the big man's knees and, tangled, Mr. Berry fell—just at the edge of the wharf. Frederick struck again; Mr. Berry raised himself to his knees and swung his fist at Jim, catching him on the ear. Jim fell, but the big man was off balance. Frederick saw his chance, and with the last of his strength swung the stick.

Mr. Berry disappeared.

Jim was lying still. Frederick fell to his knees and was

sick. Jim pulled himself to the edge and looked over. There was silence.

"Where is he?" said Frederick through thick lips and broken teeth.

"Down there," said Jim.

Frederick crawled to the edge. There was a stone platform a yard or so wide at the foot of the jetty; Mr. Berry lay sprawled half across this and half across the mud. His head was twisted horribly to one side.

"You done it," said Jim. "We done it. We killed him."

"Where's Adelaide?"

They looked around. The wharf was empty. The rain had stopped, and the puddles gleamed in the dim light. Below them on the mud the lowest boats were stirring and slowly righting themselves, as if they were rising from their graves; but it was only the tide coming in. Jim and Frederick were alone. Adelaide had gone.

18

London Bridge

MUCH LATER, SALLY AWOKE. THE HANDS OF THE kitchen clock had advanced to midnight, and the fire had burned low. Trembler was asleep in the armchair. Everything was familiar—except herself; for she had changed, and so the world had changed. She could hardly believe what had happened ... except that it explained everything.

Trembler woke up with a start.

"Good God, miss! What's the time?"

"Midnight."

"Have you—oh, no, I didn't fall asleep, did I?"

She nodded. "It doesn't matter."

"You all right, miss? I'm awful sorry—"

"No, no, I'm fine."

"You look proper shocked, as if you've seen a ghost. Let me make you a cup o' tea. And I said I'd stay awake. . . . Fat lot o' good I am."

Sally wasn't listening. Trembler got up and touched her shoulder.

"Miss?"

"I've got to find the ruby. I've got to have it."

She stood up and moved to the window, looking distracted, beating her hands together gently. Trembler stood away, alarmed, and gnawed his mustache. Then he spoke again.

"Miss, wait till Mr. Frederick gets back—"

There was a rattle at the door. Trembler sprang to unlock it, and a moment later Rosa was in the kitchen, cold and wet and cross.

"What on earth have you got the door locked for? Ugh—what a night! And the house less than half full, and a miserable bunch they were—Sally, what's the matter? What is it? What's that smell?"

She wrinkled her wet nose and brushed the water out of her eyes as she looked around and saw the ash and the matches on the table.

"What's this? Not opium?"

Trembler came in before Sally could speak. "It was my fault, Miss Rosa," he said quickly. "I let her do it."

"And what's happened to you?" She dropped her cloak on the floor and hurried to look at his bruised eye and cheek. "What in the world has been going on? Where's Fred?"

"Adelaide's gone," said Trembler. "Mrs. Holland come with some great big bruiser and snatched her in the street. Mr. Fred and that young Jim went after 'em."

"When?"

"Hours back."

"Oh my God—but Sally, why the opium?"

"I had to. Now I've got to find the ruby, because I know all about it. Oh, Rosa, I'm—"

Her voice shook, and she put her arms around Rosa and broke into a sudden sobbing. Rosa embraced her and sat her down gently.

"What is it, love? What's the trouble?"

Her cold wet hands soothed Sally's cheeks. In a moment or so Sally shook her head and sat up straight, wiping away the tears with rough fingers.

"I've got to find that ruby. That's the only way I'll ever finish this business off. I've *got* to work it out . . ."

"Wait there," said Rosa.

She ran upstairs and was back in under a minute. She dropped something on the table—something heavy, wrapped in a handkerchief; something that glinted in the linen folds.

"I don't believe it," said Trembler.

Sally looked at her in pure astonishment.

"It was Jim," Rosa explained. "He—you know these stories he's always reading—I suppose he thinks like a sensational novelist. He worked it out some time ago. It was in a pub in Swaleness, apparently—I can't remember the details—but he kept it away from you because he thought there was a curse on it and he didn't want you hurt. Do you *know* what he thinks of you, Sally? He worships you. But he brought it to me today because he thought I'd know what to do. He told me the whole story just before I left for the theater, so I didn't have time to tell you earlier on. It's Jim you've got to thank. Anyway . . . There it is."

Sally, speechless, reached out and opened the handkerchief. In the center of the crumpled whiteness was a dome of blood—a stone the size of the top joint of a man's thumb, containing all the redness in the world. It seemed to draw in the light of the nearby lamp and magnify it, and change it, and cast it out again as visible heat; and inside it was that shimmering drugged landscape of caverns, ravines, abysses, which had so mesmerized Major

Marchbanks. Sally felt her head swim and her eyelids droop . . . Then she closed her hand around it. It was hard and small and cold. She stood up.

"Trembler," she said, "take a cab now and go to Hangman's Wharf. Tell Mrs. Holland that I have the ruby, and I will meet her in the middle of London Bridge in an hour's time. That's all."

"But—"

"I'll give you the money. Do it, Trembler. You—you fell asleep while I was in my Nightmare; please do this."

A spasm crossed her face as she said this, as if she hated reminding him of his failure. He bowed his head and shuffled into his greatcoat.

Rosa jumped up.

"Sally—you can't! You mustn't! What are you thinking of?"

"I can't explain now, Rosa. But I will soon. And you'll see I've got to meet her."

"But—"

"Please, Rosa, trust me. This is the most important thing—the *only* thing that matters now—you can't understand. . . . I couldn't understand myself, before . . ."

She indicated the ashes of the opium and shuddered.

"At least let me come with you," said Rosa. "You can't go alone. Tell me on the way."

"No. I want to meet her alone. Trembler, you're not to come there yourself. Just send her."

He looked up guiltily, and then nodded and left.

Rosa went on: "I'll let you go onto the bridge alone but I'm coming as far as there with you. I think you're crazy, Sally."

"You don't know—" Sally began, but shook her head. "All right. But you promise to let me meet her alone.

You've got to promise not to interfere, whatever happens."

Rosa nodded. "All right," she said. "I'm starving. I'm going to eat a sandwich on the way."

She cut a slice of bread from the loaf on the sideboard and spread it thickly with butter and jam.

"Ready for anything," she said. "And sopping wet. You're mad, you're insane. A lunatic. Come on—it's a long walk."

SALLY HEARD the city clocks chiming the half hour: half past one. She walked slowly back and forth, ignoring the occasional pedestrian and the even more occasional cab or four-wheeler. Once a policeman stopped and asked if she was all right, evidently thinking that here was another of those poor wretches who looked to the river as the answer to all their sorrows; but she smiled and reassured him, and he walked on steadily.

A quarter of an hour passed. A cab rolled up to the rank at the northern end of the bridge, but no one got out. The driver hunched his coat up around his shoulders and dozed, waiting for a passenger. The river moved beneath her; she watched the tide flowing in, lifting the boats tied up at both banks, with their riding lights glowing. Once a police steam-launch chugged down from Southwark Bridge. She watched it come and disappear beneath her feet, and then walked across to see it come out the other side and go down slowly past the dark bulk of the Tower and curve off toward the right. She wondered if that thickly clustered shore on the left was Wapping, and if so, which of those black wharves backed onto Holland's Lodgings.

Time passed; she got colder. The clocks chimed again.

And then a figure appeared under the gaslight at the northern end of the bridge—a squat, dumpy figure in black.

Sally straightened, and a yawn died away in her throat. She stood in the middle of the pavement, clear of the parapet, so as to be seen, and in a moment the figure began to move toward her. It could only be Mrs. Holland; Sally saw her clearly. Even at this distance, the old woman's eyes seemed to glitter. She moved in and out of alternate shadow and light, limping a little, wheezing, holding her side, but never stopping.

She came to within three yards of Sally and stopped. The ancient crooked bonnet she wore obscured the top part of her face so that only her mouth and chin could be seen clearly, her mouth working all the time as if she were chewing something small and resistant; but still the eyes glittered in the darkness.

"Well, dear?" she said at last.

"You killed my father."

Mrs. Holland's mouth opened a little, exposing the great sheet of teeth. A pointed, leathery tongue crawled slowly across them and withdrew.

"Well," she said. "You can't make accusations of that kind, missy."

"I know all about it. I know that Major Marchbanks—that Major Marchbanks was my father. He was, wasn't he?"

Silence from Mrs. Holland.

"And he sold me, didn't he? He sold me to Captain Lockhart, the man I thought . . . the man I knew as my father. He sold me for the ruby."

Mrs. Holland was perfectly still, perfectly silent.

"Because the maharajah gave the ruby to my—to Captain Lockhart as payment for protecting him during the mutiny. That's right, isn't it?"

Slowly the old woman nodded.

"Because the rebels thought he was helping the British. And my f—and Captain Lockhart left Major Marchbanks guarding the maharajah in—in the dark somewhere—"

"The Residency cellars," said Mrs. Holland. "With the women—some of 'em. And the children—some of 'em."

"And Major Marchbanks had been smoking opium— and he was afraid and ran away and they killed the maharajah and when he came back with my—with Captain Lockhart . . . they quarreled. Major Marchbanks begged for the ruby. He had debts and he couldn't pay them—"

"The opium. Pitiful. It was opium as killed him."

"*You* killed him!"

"Now, now. I want that ruby, miss. That's what I come for. I got a right to it."

"You can have it—when you tell me the rest of the truth."

"How do I know you got it?"

For answer Sally took the handkerchief out of her bag and set it on the parapet under the gaslight. She unwrapped the ruby so that it sat, red on white, in the very center of the broad stone ledge. Mrs. Holland took an involuntary step toward it.

"One more step and it goes over," said Sally. "The truth. I know enough now to be able to tell if you're lying. I want it all."

Mrs. Holland faced her again.

"All right," she said. "You got it right. They came back and found the maharajah dead, and Lockhart knocked

Marchbanks down for a coward. Then he heard the child crying. You, that was. Marchbank's wife had died—sickly thing. Lockhart says, is this pore child going to grow up with a coward for a father? A coward and an opium-smoker? Take the ruby, he says. Take it and be damned, but give me the child . . ."

She stopped. Sally heard the heavy tread of the police-man returning. Neither of the women moved; the ruby lay on the parapet, in plain view. The policeman stopped.

"All right, ladies?"

"Yes, thank you," said Sally.

"Nasty night to be out. We're going to have more rain, I shouldn't wonder."

"Wouldn't be surprised," said Mrs. Holland.

"I should get off indoors if I was you. I wouldn't be out meself if I didn't have to be, eh? Well, back to the beat."

He touched his helmet and walked on.

"Go on," said Sally.

"So Marchbanks snatches the child—that's you—from the cradle and gives it to Lockhart. It was the opium and the debts working in his mind. And he pockets the ruby, and—that's all."

"No, it isn't. What did Captain Lockhart's wife say?"

"Wife? He never had a wife. He was a bachelor."

And that was Sally's mother gone. Wiped away at a stroke: and it was almost the worst blow of all to know that that wonderful, vital woman had never even existed.

Sally said shakily, "But I've got a scar on my arm. A bullet—"

"That was no bullet; that was a knife. The same knife as killed the maharajah, rot his soul. They was going to kill you, only they was disturbed."

Sally felt faint. "Well, go on," she said. "What about you? How do you come into it? Don't forget, I know some of it, and if you don't tell the truth—"

She took hold of the corner of the handkerchief. It was a lie: she had no idea of how Mrs. Holland was involved, but from the old woman's gasp as Sally reached for the ruby, Sally knew she would get the truth.

"It was me husband," she said hoarsely. "Horatio. He was a soldier in the regiment, and he got wind of it."

"How?" said Sally, and pushed the stone closer to the edge.

"He was down there," said Mrs. Holland swiftly, her hands twisting around each other in her anxiety. "He saw it and heard it. And later on, back home—"

"So you blackmailed him. Major Marchbanks, my real father. You robbed him of everything. Didn't you?"

"He was ashamed. Bitter ashamed. Course he didn't want no one to hear about what he done. Sell his own child for a jewel? Dreadful."

"But why do you say the ruby is yours? If the maharajah gave it to Captain Lockhart, and he gave it to Major Marchbanks, what right have you got to it?"

"I got the best right of any of you. He promised it to me hisself twenty years before, the lying bastard. He promised it."

"Who? My father?"

"No—the maharajah!"

"What? Why? Whatever for?"

"He was in love with me."

Sally laughed. The idea was preposterous; the old woman was making it up.

But Mrs. Holland shook her fist in fury, and hissed,

"It's true! So help me God I made a bargain with you, missy, the truth for the ruby, and this is God's own truth. You look at me now and you think I'm old and ugly, but twenty years before the mutiny—before I married—I were the loveliest lass in the whole o' northern India. Pretty Molly Beckwith, they used to call me. My father were the company farrier in Agrapur—only a humble civilian, but they all came to pay their respects, the officers, and make eyes at me—and not only the officers, neither. The maharajah hisself fell for me, damn him. You know what he wanted. . . . He were crazy with love for me, and I'd toss me head at him—a head full o' dark curls. . . . You think you're pretty; you're a washed-out mournful thing beside the girl I was. You're nothing, you are. You'd never compare. Well, the maharajah promised me the ruby. So I gave in. And then he laughed and threw me out of the palace; and I never saw the ruby again till that night in the Residency cellars—"

"It was you who saw everything, then! Not your husband!"

"What's it matter now? Yes, I saw it all. More than that: I let in the men who killed him. And I laughed as he died . . ."

She smiled at the memory. Sally could see nothing of the beauty she claimed to have had. There was nothing left at all—nothing but age and cruelty. And yet Sally believed her, and almost felt sorry—until she remembered Major Marchbanks, and his strange timid gentleness the day they had met, the way he had looked at the girl he knew was his daughter. . . . No, she did not feel sorry.

So she took the ruby in her hand.

"And is that all the truth?"

"All that matters. Come on—it's mine. Mine before you, before your father, before Lockhart. I was bought with that stone—same as you. The pair of us, each bought for a ruby. . . . Now give it to me."

"I don't want it," said Sally. "It's brought nothing but death and unhappiness. My father meant me to have it and not you, but I don't want it. I give up all my claim to it. And if you want it"—she held it up—"you can go and get it."

And she threw it over the parapet.

Mrs. Holland stood perfectly still.

They both heard the faint splash far below as the stone hit the water; and then Mrs. Holland went mad.

First, she laughed and tossed her head like a young girl, and patted it with satisfaction as if there were not a filthy old bonnet there but a mass of dark, glossy curls.

Then she said, "My beauty. My pretty Molly. You shall have a ruby for your lovely arms, for your blue eyes, for your red lips . . ."

Then her teeth fell out. She took no notice, but her speech became incoherent, and her bonnet fell crookedly, obscuring half her face. She thrust Sally aside and scrambled up onto the parapet. She tottered wildly for a moment; Sally, horrified, put out a hand, but felt only the empty air as the old woman plunged.

She fell without a cry. Sally put her hands over her ears; she felt rather than heard the impact of Mrs. Holland's body hitting the water.

Sally sank to her knees and cried.

And at the northern end of the bridge, the driver of the cab flicked his whip gently and shook the reins, and the cab began to move.

It came at a walk along the roadway and stopped beside her. She was still sobbing; she looked up through a mist of tears. The driver's face was hidden, the occupant—if there was one—invisible.

The door opened. A hand rested on it—a large sunburned hand, with fair hair on the back and knuckles. A voice she had never heard before said: "Please get into the cab, Miss Lockhart. We have something to discuss."

She stood up, speechless. She still shook from time to time with sobs, but that was automatic: she was now devastated with astonishment.

"Who are you?" she managed to say.

"I have many names. I recently visited Oxford under the name of Eliot. The other day I had an appointment with Mr. Selby, and the name I used then was Todd. In the East I am sometimes known as Ah Ling; but my real name is Hendrik Van Eeden. Into the cab, Miss Lockhart."

Sally was in a state beyond surprise, beyond resistance. Like a helpless child she climbed into the cab. Van Eeden shut the door, and they moved away.

19

The East India Docks

SALLY HELD HER BAG TIGHTLY ON HER LAP. INSIDE IT, loaded, was the gun she had bought for the enemy she could not see. And here he was . . . She felt the cab turn right as it left the bridge and moved down Lower Thames Street toward the Tower. She sat trembling in a corner, hardly able to breathe for fear.

The man said nothing and did not move. She could feel his eyes on her, and her skin crawled. The cab turned left and began to move through a maze of smaller streets which were less well lit.

"Where are we going?" she said shakily.

"To the East India Docks," he said. "And then you may come farther, or you may stay."

His voice was soft and cracked. He spoke without trace of any accent, but he shaped each word carefully, as if he were remembering how to say it.

"I don't understand," she said.

He smiled.

She could see his face dimly in the inconstant light from the gas lamps they passed. It was broad and genial; but his eyes, glistening darkly, traversed her slowly from head to toe. She felt as if he were touching her, and shrank away into the corner and shut her eyes.

The cab turned right, into the Commercial Road. He lit a cheroot and filled the cab with smoke; it made her feel sick and dizzy.

"Please," she said, "may I open a window?"

"I beg your pardon," he said. "How thoughtless of me."

He unfastened the window on his side and threw out the cheroot. Sally slipped her hand into the bag as he did so, but he turned back before she had found the gun. Neither of them spoke. The only sound was the trundling of the wheels on the road and the clop of the horse's hooves.

Several minutes passed. She looked out of the window. They were passing the Limehouse Basin of the Regent's Canal, and she saw the masts of ships and the gleam of a night watchman's fire. And then they were past and turning into the East India Dock Road. Somewhere in the night not far from here was Madame Chang.... Would she help, if Sally could get to her? But she would never remember the way.

Her hand crept, little by little, farther into the bag and closer to the gun. And her heart sank, for it had been raining hard during her walk to London Bridge, and the bag was soaked. *Please let the powder be dry....*

Ten more minutes passed in silence, and the cab turned into a narrow street bounded by a factory on one side and a high wall on the other. The only light came from a single gaslight at the corner of the street. The cab pulled up to the pavement and stopped, and Van Eeden leaned out of the window and gave some money to the driver. Without a word, the driver got down and unharnessed the horse. Sally felt the cab rock as he climbed down, and heard the jingle of the harness, and felt the little jolt as the shafts were laid on the ground; and then she heard the faint clop of the horse's hooves as the driver led it away and around the corner. And then there was silence again.

Sally had found the pistol. It was pointing the wrong way; under cover of shifting her position, she turned the bag around and gripped the handle. Everything felt so damp . . .

"We have a little more than half an hour," said Van Eeden. "There is a ship beyond that wall which is going to sail with the tide. I am going with it. You may come, alive, or you may stay here, dead."

"I don't understand."

He smiled.

"I was going to kill you straight away, of course. But I have been watching you, and I think it would be a waste. You are brave and resourceful. You would be useful to me. Also, you are beautiful. Not as beautiful as a Chinese woman, of course, but sufficiently good-looking to give me pleasure. I am offering you your life, Miss Lockhart. Think about it."

She felt sick.

"But why did you kill my father?" she asked, playing for time.

"Because he interfered in the affairs of my society."

"The Seven Blessings?"

"Precisely."

"But how can you belong to a Chinese secret society? Aren't you Dutch?"

"Oh, partly. It is my fate to look more like my father than my mother, but my ancestry is not in question. My mother, you see, was the daughter of Ling Chi, who earned his living in a traditional and praiseworthy way—you would call it piracy. What is more natural than that I should seek to follow the example of my illustrious grandfather? I had the benefits of a European education, so I was able to obtain a post as agent to a well-known firm dealing with the shipping trade, and then to set up an arrangement beneficial to both parties."

"Both parties?"

"The firm of Lockhart and Selby, and the Seven Blessings Society. It was opium which provided the link. Your father refused to deal in it—a shortsighted and pointless policy, in my view, and one which led to his death. No, I was pleased with the arrangement I created, and annoyed when he threatened to ruin it."

"What was this arrangement?" said Sally. Her thumb was on the hammer; would the warmth of her hand dry the powder? And would the barrel hold, even if it did fire?

"The finest opium," Van Eeden went on, "comes from India, grown under British government supervision, and there is an official stamp, you know, a sort of mold, to form the stuff into little official cakes with Her Majesty's blessing and approval. Very civilized. It commands a ready sale and a high price. Unfortunately, your father would not deal in it, so Lockhart and Selby were not in a position to benefit from it.

"So in my capacity as Ah Ling, I made a practice of intercepting vessels carrying opium from India. It is the work of a morning to persuade the crew to cooperate; the work of an afternoon to transfer the cargo to my junk; the work of an agreeable evening to sink their ship and sail away."

"And then Lockhart and Selby take the stolen opium and sell it, I suppose?" said Sally. "Very clever. A credit to you."

"Far too obvious. It would be spotted at once. No, here comes the beauty of the scheme. By a lucky chance, my society came into the possession of one of those very valuable British government stamps. So with the help of the stamp and a factory in Penang, together with some low-grade opium from the hills, one shipload becomes three or four, all stamped and certified and shipped by that most respectable firm, Lockhart and Selby."

"You adulterate it. . . . And what happens to those who smoke the opium?"

"They die. In the case of those who smoke our altered opium, they die more quickly, which is a blessing for them. It was most unwise of your father to intervene; it gave me a lot of trouble. I was in Penang in the character of Hendrik Van Eeden; I had to become Ah Ling and arrive at Singapore before your father left. . . . Devilish difficult. But the gods have been kind. It is nearly over."

He took a watch from his waistcoat pocket.

"Admirable time," he said. "Well, Miss Lockhart, have you decided? Do you come, or do you stay?"

She looked down and saw, with horror, the open blade of a knife in his lap. It glinted in the faint light from the dockyard over the wall. His voice was soft and thick as if he spoke through felt, and she found herself beginning to shake. *No, no, be still,* she told herself. But this wasn't a target pinned to a wall—this was a living man, and it would kill him . . .

She pulled back the hammer with her thumb. It made a faint click.

Van Eeden leaned forward and caressed her hand

briefly. She drew it away, but he was swifter: one hand flew to her mouth, the other held the knife to her breast. The hand over her mouth was sweetly scented; she felt sick and pushed the bag up between them, an inch from his chest. She heard his breathing. She was dizzy with fear.

"Well?" he said softly.

And then she squeezed the trigger.

THE EXPLOSION seemed to rock the cab. The impact flung Van Eeden away from her and back against the seat; the knife dropped from his hand, and he clutched at his chest and opened his mouth once or twice, trying to say something—and then he slipped to the floor and fell still.

She opened the door and ran. She threw herself forward, away from what she had done; she was crying, she was shaking, she was wild with fear . . .

She couldn't see where she was going. There were footsteps coming after her, running, pursuing.

Someone was calling her name. She cried "No! No!" and ran on. She found she was clutching the gun, and flung it from herself with loathing; it skittered over the wet cobbles and then disappeared into the gutter.

A hand caught her arm.

"Sally! Stop! Sally, don't! Listen! Look—it's me—"

She fell and all the breath was knocked out of her. She twisted to look up, and saw Rosa.

"Rosa—oh, Rosa, what have I done—"

She clung to her and sobbed, and Rosa held her tightly and rocked her like a child, kneeling heedlessly in the filthy gutter.

"Sally, Sally—I heard a shot and—are you hurt? What has he done?"

"I k-k-killed him—I killed him—it was m-me—"

And then came a fresh burst of sobbing. Rosa held her more tightly and stroked her hair.

"Are you—did you—are you sure?" she said, looking over Sally's shoulder.

"I shot him, Rosa," said Sally, her face in Rosa's neck. "Because he was going to—going to kill me, and . . . He had a knife . . ."

Such floods of grief shook her now that Rosa felt herself weeping too. She could not speak.

But eventually the older girl pulled her gently upright.

"Listen, Sally," she said, "we must find a policeman. We've got to—don't shake your head—we absolutely must. It's gone too far now. And with Mrs. Holland and everything. . . . You mustn't worry. It's all finished. But now that it's over, we must go to the police. I know what happened—I can testify to it. You won't get into trouble."

"I didn't know you were there," said Sally weakly, standing up and looking down at the mud on her cloak and skirt.

"How could I let you just go off like that? I got into another cab and followed. Thank heaven there was one there. And when I heard the shot—"

She shook her head; and then they heard the sound of a police whistle.

Sally looked at her.

"That's from the cab," she said. "They must have found him. Come on. . . ."

20

The Clock Tower

STRANGE EVENTS AT EAST INDIA DOCKS

MYSTERY OF EMPTY CAB

A SHOT IN THE NIGHT

An unexplained and mysterious disturbance took place near the East India Docks during the early hours of the morning of Tuesday last.

Police Constable Jonas Torrance, an experienced and reliable officer, was patroling his beat in the area of the docks when, at approximately twenty minutes past two, he heard the sound of a shot.

He hastened to make a search of the area, and within five minutes had found a four-wheeler cab apparently abandoned in East India Dock Wall Road. There was no sign of horse or driver, but when the constable looked inside the cab, he found evidence of a desperate struggle.

On the floor and seat was a substantial quantity of blood. P.C. Torrance estimated it to be not less than three pints and possibly a great deal more. It is clear that no one could lose this amount of blood in so short a time and live;

222

and yet nowhere could be found the victim of this brutal attack.

A closer examination of the cab revealed a knife, of the sort used by seamen, under one of the seats. The blade was prodigiously sharp, but it was clean and free of blood.

The constable summoned aid, and a search was made of the neighboring streets, but nothing further was discovered. At present the case remains a mystery.

"We tried to tell him," said Sally. "Didn't we, Rosa?"

"We told him four times, and he wouldn't listen. Not a word would penetrate his skull. He ordered us away in the end, and said that we were hindering him in the performance of his duty."

"He just refused to believe it."

"He's an experienced and reliable officer," said Frederick. "It says so here. I think he had every right to send you about your business, and I don't know what you're complaining of. Do you, Bedwell?"

They were sitting around the table in Burton Street. It was three days later; the Reverend Bedwell had come down from Oxford to learn what had happened, and had accepted their invitation to dinner. Rosa was there because the play she was in had been taken off: the backer had lost his nerve before he had recovered his money, and Rosa was out of a job as a consequence. Sally knew that the Burton Street economy would suffer badly, but had said nothing.

Mr. Bedwell thought before answering Frederick's question.

"It seems to me you did the right thing in going to him," he said. "That was entirely good and proper. And you tried to tell him—what, four times?"

Rosa nodded. "He thought we were just being foolish and wasting his time."

"Then I think you've done all that you need to, and his reply is no more than the blindness of justice. The outcome is just; he was shot in self-defense, after all, which is a right we all have. And there's no trace of the man now?"

"Not a sign," said Frederick. "He probably found his way back to his ship. He's either dead or on his way to the East by now."

Mr. Bedwell nodded. "Well, Miss Lockhart, I think you've done everything you should, and your conscience should be perfectly clear."

Frederick said quietly, "What about me? I intended to kill that ruffian of Mrs. Holland's. In fact, I told him I would. Was that murder?"

"In defense of another, your actions were justified. As for your intentions—of that, I can't judge. You may have to live with the knowledge that you set out to kill a man. But I've exchanged blows with the fellow myself, and I wouldn't judge you too harshly."

Frederick's face was badly bruised. His nose had been broken, and he had lost three teeth; and his hands were so painful that he still had great difficulty in holding anything. Sally, when she saw him, had cried. She cried very easily now.

"How's the young fellow?" Mr. Bedwell went on.

"Jim? A broken arm and a fine pair of black eyes and assorted bruises. But you'd have to attack him with a regiment of cavalry and a howitzer or two to do any serious damage. What I'm more concerned about is the fact that he's lost his job."

"The firm's closed down," said Sally. "It's in utter confusion. There's a report about it on another page of today's paper."

"And the little girl?"

"Nothing," said Rosa. "Not a word. Not a sign. We've looked everywhere—we've been to all the orphanages—but she's vanished."

She did not voice what they all feared.

"My poor brother was very fond of her," said the clergyman. "She kept him alive in that horrible place. . . . Well, well; we must hope. But as for you, Miss Lockhart—well, should I call you Miss Lockhart? Or Miss Marchbanks?"

"I've been Lockhart for sixteen years. And when I hear the word *father*, I think of Mr. Lockhart. I don't know what legal status I have, or what rubies count for in courts of law . . . I'm Sally Lockhart. I work for a photographer. That's all that matters now."

BUT IT WASN'T. A week went by, and still Adelaide did not appear, in spite of Trembler's endless tramping the streets and inquiring at the schools and workhouses. And still Rosa did not find another job, and worse: the play she had been rehearsing for folded too. Now there was nothing coming in at all except for what they could sell in the shop, and that situation was almost the worst of all—for having begun to establish themselves and sell the pictures, they needed desperately to build on this first foundation before the public lost interest; and they had no money to pay for the new pictures they would have to produce.

Sally tried one supplier after another, but no one would let them have paper or chemicals on credit. She argued, she pleaded, she put the case as forcibly as she could, and got next to nothing. One firm let them have some printing paper, but not enough; that was the only success they had. As for the printing firm who was going to produce the stereographs, they had refused to pay any money in advance, and any royalties they could look forward to were too far ahead in the future to be of any use now. At one point Sally had to stop Frederick from selling the studio camera. "Don't sell the equipment," she told him; "never do that. How on earth would we get it back? What are we going to do when we expand, if we have to spend the first money we get on buying back equipment we should never have let go in the first place?" He saw the sense of it, and the camera stayed in the studio. Occasionally he took a portrait or two; but the business they all cherished was dying.

And Sally knew that she had the money to save it. And she knew that if she tried to use it, Mr. Temple would find her and stop her, and she would lose everything.

Finally, one cold, still morning at the end of November, a letter arrived from Oxford:

Dear Miss Lockhart,

I must ask you to forgive my lapse of memory. I can only put it down to the shock of my poor brother's death, and the tragic events we have all lived through. Perhaps it is not important anyway, but I am sure you would want to know that before he died, Matthew remembered something your father—Captain Lockhart, that is—had said to him on the night the *Lavinia* was sunk. It was part of the message he had come all this way to deliver, poor fellow.

Captain Lockhart had said: "Tell her to look under the clock."

That was all Matthew remembered, but he insisted I

write it down and tell you. I did the first, but forgot the second until now.

I hope it has some meaning for you. Once again, I must apologize for not remembering it sooner.

> With my kindest regards,
> Yours very truly,
> Nicholas Bedwell

Sally felt her heart beating fast. She knew which clock he meant. Their house in Norwood had, over the stable, a wooden clocktower—a tiny little folly cheerfully carved and painted, with a clock that struck the quarters and needed winding once a week. It was a preposterous thing to have in a suburban villa, but Sally had loved to clamber about the loft above the stable and watch the mechanism beating slowly. And underneath the clock there was a loose plank in the wooden wall of the loft, which Sally had prized off one day to find a perfect hiding place for treasures.

Look under the clock . . .

Well, it might be nothing, but it was all she had left. Without saying anything to the others, she bought a train ticket and set off for Norwood.

The house had changed in the four months since she had last seen it. The windows and the door had been painted, there was a new iron gate, and the rosebed in the center of the circular drive had been dug up and replaced with what looked as if it was going to be a fountain. It was not her home anymore, and she was glad of that; the past was over and finished.

The tenants were a Mr. and Mrs. Green and their large

family. Mr. Green was at work when Sally arrived—somewhere in the city—and Mrs. Green was paying a call on a neighbor, but a friendly, harassed governess saw Sally at once, and raised no objections to her looking in the stables.

"Of course they won't mind," she said. "They're very kind—Charles! Stop that at once!" (Sally noticed that a small child was demolishing an umbrella stand.) "Please go ahead, Miss Lockhart—do excuse me, but I must—Oh, Charles, really!—You can find your own way? Of course you can."

The stables had not changed, and the familiar smell and the sound of the clock gave her a brief pang; but she hadn't come for that. It took her only a minute to make her way up to the hiding place and find the box—a little rosewood chest, bound with brass, which had stood on her father's desk for years. She recognized it at once and drew it out.

She sat on the dusty floor to open it. There was no key, just a simple catch.

The box was full of bank notes.

It took her several moments to realize what she had in her hands. She touched them wonderingly; she couldn't even guess how much there was. And then she saw a letter.

22 June 1872

My dearest Sally,

If you are reading this, the worst has happened, and I am dead. My poor girl, you'll have so much to bear—but you've got the strength to do it.

This money, darling, is for you. It is exactly to the penny the sum I put into Lockhart and Selby years ago, when Selby was a good man. The firm will crash soon. I have made sure of that. But I have recovered this, and it is yours.

I am going to the East because an evil thing has wound itself around the company, and I must deal with it. No doubt I was a fool not to have spotted it earlier, but I trusted Selby, and—I repeat—he was a good man once.

That evil thing, Sally, is opium. All the China trade we now have was founded on it. The British government trades in it. But I thought for years that Lockhart and Selby did not; I would not allow it to, because I hate it.

I do so because I saw what it did to George Marchbanks, once my closest friend. If you are reading this, my dear one, you will have found your way to him by one means or another; you will know who he is, and what bargain we made. I have not seen him from that day to this, but I know he is still alive, and I know he will tell you the truth if you go to him.

As for the ruby—perhaps he still has it, perhaps not. It is a horrible thing, tainted with blood and murder—and with the very evil I am going to seek out, because the wealth that paid for it in the first place came from the poppy fields of Agrapur. Those fields are today more prosperous than ever; the evil remains.

But I am hopeful. We have a good agent in Singapore, a man called Van Eeden. I shall talk to him, and together we shall deal with this corruption.

Take the money, my Sally, and forgive me. Forgive me for not telling you to your face; and forgive me for inventing your mother. There was a girl like that, and I loved her, but she married another man; and she is long dead.

I give you the money in cash, because I know how long it would take you to extract it from the grasp of a lawyer. Temple is a good man and will look after the rest of your money faithfully and well, but he'll consider you incapable of doing so yourself, and he'll use every method the laws of

England allow him to keep it out of your hands—for the best of motives. But with cash, you have freedom. Look for a small business, one which needs capital to expand. You will do it. You will choose well. I have chosen less happily; my friends, my partner, all have disappointed me.

But once in my life I chose very well. It was when I chose you, my dear one, in preference to a fortune. That choice has been my greatest pride and my greatest joy. Good-bye, my Sally. You will understand what it means when I sign myself with the deepest love,

> Your father,
> Matthew Lockhart

She let the paper fall and bowed her head. Everything had come to this now: to a box full of money, and a letter. She was crying. She had loved him very much, real father or not . . .

And he had made everything safe; there would be a future.

"Daddy," she whispered.

Oh, there would be difficulties, hundreds of them. But she would cope.

She gathered up letter and box and left for the train.

Philip Pullman

was born in Norwich, England, and was brought up in Rhodesia, Australia, London, and Wales. He earned a degree in English from Oxford University, and since 1973 has taught in the Oxford schools while writing a novel for adults (*Galatea*), a Gothic comedy for children (*Count Karlstein*), a play (*Sherlock Holmes and the Adventure of the Sumatran Devil*), and two books for young adults—*The Ruby in the Smoke* and its sequel, *The Shadow on the Plate*. He is currently working on a third novel to complete the trilogy.

Mr. Pullman lives with his wife and four children in Oxford, England.

YA
F
PUL

22198

Pullman, Philip

The ruby in the
smoke

DATE DUE

NOV 1 4 '87	NOV 1 7 1997	NOV 1 4 2008
JAN 9 '88		2-15-13
AUG 2 0 '88	JUN 1 5 1998	
DEC 1 9 1990		May 15 14
MAR 0 1 1991	SEP 1 6 1998	
AUG 0 7 1991	AUG 2 3 1999	
SEP 0 4 1991		
JAN 3 1 1992	AUG 2 9 2001	
FEB 1 3 1993	JUN 1 9 2005	
FEB 0 2 '96	JAN 2 8 2006	
AUG 2 4 1996		
SEP 0 6 2002	JUL 1 9 2007	
APR 0 5 2005		